A CHRISTMAS CHARM
Copyright © 2022 by Gretchen Rose

ISBN: 979-8-88653-082-7

Published by Satin Romance
An Imprint of Melange Books, LLC
White Bear Lake, MN 55110
www.satinromance.com

Published in the United States of America.

Cover Design by Caroline Andrus

A Christmas Charm

GRETCHEN ROSE

CONTENTS

ANNABELLE & FRIENDS' HOLIDAY RECIPES

This book is dedicated to Mel Laracey, who gave me a second chance at love and happiness.

Special thanks to my dear sister, Amy Schade, and good friends, Anne Alexander and Jane Gennarelli, who provided some of Annabelle Bow's holiday recipes.

And to my mother, Barbara, who so loved Christmas. She was an inspiration to all, celebrating the holiday season with style, beauty, and grace.

"I truly believe that if we keep telling the Christmas story, singing the Christmas songs, and living the Christmas spirit, we can bring joy and happiness and peace to this world."

— NORMAN VINCENT PEALE

"I will honour Christmas in my heart and try to keep it all the year."

— CHARLES DICKENS, *A CHRISTMAS CAROL*

ONE
AWAY AND AWAY

Olivia Barone had no idea how this hastily conceived breakout would end, and a feeling of reckless giddiness washed over her. The terror that had driven her to this new reality, worlds away from the hustle and bustle of New York City and its frenetic traffic, slowly loosened its grip on her heart, and she let her eyes drift from the two lane-highway spooling out before her to the close-cropped fields abutting it. It was late in the afternoon, but the sun shone brightly in an azure sky, painting the surrounding meadows and pastures in techno color. Lovely! How long had it been since she'd had the time to appreciate the glorious countryside?

The farmland stretched before her like an enormous patchwork quilt, every plot and rise a different pattern and complexion. Recently harvested, they were either brown or golden and stubbled, or feathery green, with tender blades of newly germinated winter wheat. In the distance, scraped and naked plots were abutted by wooded copses ablaze in their autumnal finery. It was a time of transition.

How fitting.

She jabbed a button, and the Beemer's convertible top folded in upon itself, retracting behind the back seat where a guitar perched atop a jumble of bags and suitcases, remainders of an interrupted and most unsatisfactory life. Oliva tossed her head, and the wind threaded through her auburn tresses as she breathed in the intoxicating scent of woodfire and freedom.

In the next instant, the tiny dog in her lap stirred, and she ran a hand down his once black but now silvery silken coat. "Hey there, Milo," she murmured. "Feels good to be out of Dodge. Doesn't it?"

The Yorkshire terrier gazed up at her with limpid brown eyes that could melt the most hardened heart. He'd never been one for small talk, but she got the drift.

"Yep. I thought so, too." She pressed the AM button and a rich baritone, radio-voice boomed from the speakers.

"Howdy, folks. Rhett Dunbar here, bringing it to you at 1370 on your AM dial. It's another gorgeous day out there, and I hope you're enjoying the last of our Indian summer because it's not going to last much longer, my friends. No siree. Temps are predicted to plummet Saturday night. There's even a chance of snow in the forecast. And speaking of predictions, Ron and Tatiana Graybar have forecast great savings on both new and used models; they're making an offer you can't refuse. Stop in at Graybar Chevrolet this weekend, test drive one of their bea-U-ti-ful cars and register for a free turkey. That's right, a plump and juicy Tom for your Thanksgiving feast. Need a car, think Graybar, where the best deals are.

"This pre-holiday weekend is cram-packed with events you won't want to miss. Fun starts Friday at 6 p.m. when the Crystal Falls Elks Club sponsors their annual fish fry to benefit the Samaritan center. There'll be live music for your dancing pleasure and the lightest, sweetest fried perch ever to tingle your taste buds. Um-mm. Makes my mouth water just thinking about it. As an added bonus, yours truly will be on hand to sign first editions of my latest collection of tunes, *America Sings*."

The radio voice crooned over a guitar accompaniment, presumably his own. "My country tis of thee..."

It was corny but pleasing, and Olivia bobbed her head to the melody of this countrified arrangement of America's national anthem. She couldn't remember when she'd last felt so carefree. Flipping down the visor, Olivia raised her sunglasses to examine her reflection in the mirror.

"Not so bad," she murmured, gently patting the bruised and puffy flesh ringing her left eye. In the next instant, a loud honking drew her gaze back to the roadway. Unnerved, she tossed the sunglasses aside.

She'd drifted into the lane of oncoming traffic. A monstrous tractor-trailer had appeared out of nowhere and was on a collision course!

Instinctively, Olivia reached for Milo. Why had she not strapped him in? A fleeting thought: if she made it out of this, she'd surely be slapped with a fine for not having restrained him. But in the next moment, she put both hands on the wheel. She needed to maneuver the powerful driving machine with all the skill she could muster. Air brakes shrilled, a horn blared, and adrenaline spiked through Olivia's veins, stabbing her heart with needle-like pricks. She jerked the wheel sharply to the right, and the semi shrieked past her with mere inches to spare.

But she was not yet out of harm's way.

She'd overcompensated!

The BMW veered crazily toward the shoulder, and she reacted by tugging the wheel in the opposite direction. The automobile responded by fishtailing out of control, two wheels on the asphalt two on the shoulder, and Olivia had all she could do to keep her grip on a steering wheel that had become a rogue jackhammer in her hands.

"Take the wheel, Jesus!" she screamed.

The Yorkie quavered in her lap, and the next few moments played out in nightmarishly slow motion. Then a sense of calm settled over her, and Olivia willed the automobile to succumb to her control.

It didn't work!

Untamed, the car spun to the right, skittering across the pavement and jouncing over rumble strips. With one hand, Olivia clutched the dog to her chest. Jolted and shaken, despite the seat belt restraint, her teeth chattered so that she feared her fillings dislodging. Too forcefully, Olivia again hit the brakes, and the car careened to the left, slewing precariously on the driver's side tires. Then, the unimaginable happened: the late-model coupe skidded out over a rise in the crumbling embankment and took flight.

Airborne, Olivia squeezed her eyes shut and prayed for deliverance. But before she could be transported to the next life, the car thudded back to Earth with such force her foot bounced off the brake. In the next moment, she found herself thrust into a harrowing game of dodge-the-hay-bales. Wild-eyed, she managed to steer the car between this confounding maze as prickly straw rained down on them like confetti. Milo barked frenziedly, adding to the confusion. But after what seemed an eternity, but was only a matter of seconds, Olivia's foot found the brake and the car slowed to a stop.

Dazed, she spat bits of straw from her mouth while eying the tightly compacted bale that filled her line of vision. It was the size of a Volkswagen Beetle and as unyielding as a brick wall. "Whew, just nicked it," she muttered as realization dawned.

She'd been spared!

Relief washed over her, and she let out a joyous whoop. "Woo-hoo! How about that, Milo, huh? What a rush! We made it, boy."

Milo licked her nose by way of answer. But then he turned from her and growled, a low menacing rumble.

"Hey, what's the matter, buddy?" Olivia peered up over a dashboard strewn with straw. Only then did she see it in the distance, a figure on horseback. He was in the open meadow abutting the hayfield, a little more than three football fields away.

"Oh no," she wailed softly, at the same time plucking chaff from her hair in a vain attempt to make herself presentable.

The rider fast approached, and she could discern another figure streaking ahead of him, some animal, a dog most likely. They were just silhouettes, and she couldn't make out any details.

She fumbled for the sunglasses that had fallen from her face. Finding them, she shoved them back on, grateful for this small gift from the universe.

"Here comes the cavalry," she groaned. "Right on cue." But then a more sinister thought pierced her consciousness: *Maybe he's pissed at me for landing in his hayfield?* "Yikes!"

4

No sooner were her words out than the pair were a mere three hale bales away.

The animal turned out to be a good-natured, golden Labrador retriever, which was a blessing, as Milo had morphed into a miniature version of a bad-assed pit bull. He scrambled off her lap and lunged to the passenger side of the car. Fangs bared, the tiny mutt snarled ferociously as the Lab slowed his pace and loped toward them.

"Milo, hush," Olivia cried.

But the pup refused to stand down. He had become her defender, and despite his size, he appeared up for the task.

Before she knew whether he was friend or foe, the horseback rider leaped from his saddle with the dexterity of a charro and strode toward her in boots up to his elbows and a chin just prominent enough to keep him from looking downright pretty.

"Are you all right?" he asked, giving her the once over. Then he repeated the exercise, only this time more slowly.

Olivia was mortified. She knew she looked a mess, and her dog's barking had ratcheted up to a hysterical pitch. The good news was the fellow appeared solicitous and to wish her no ill will. "Milo, stop!"

Through it all, the larger dog remained copasetic. He merely huffed a half-hearted reply, trotted over to the car, and tilted his head as if to ask, "Why the commotion, little guy?"

That gesture seemed to have a calming effect on Milo, and he quieted.

Olivia exhaled and her shoulders sagged. "Yeah. We're fine," she said, levering the car door open. "Whew! Just a tad shaken up is all."

Like a torpedo, the terrier shot out of the vehicle, making a beeline for the Lab. He bounced on his hind legs and put his small face up to the Labrador's huge one, nose to snout. Hulking in comparison to the wee pooch, the bigger canine, stoically endured this diminutive annoyance. Then, after politely sniffing one another, both fore and aft, the two dogs appeared to decide they were to be friends. They broke away, faced off, and then tore around in circles, feinting and lunging, the Lab ever careful not to trod on his new toy.

"Oh, brother," Olivia groaned. She turned back to her surprise would-be rescuer. He was staring, fixated on her.

Their eyes met.

The long-limbed fellow dropped the reins to his horse, and the white filly ambled off to graze.

Olivia tore her gray-green gaze from the man's sapphire blue one. "Milo, come here," she cried, but the Yorkie ignored her. He was intent on his new best buddy.

"Let them be," the man said. "They'll tire of that soon enough."

Who was this guy?

Not only was he movie-star gorgeous, but he also boasted an aura of confidence that she found incredibly sexy.

"You must think I'm a complete idiot," Olivia babbled, once more getting lost in the man's baby blues.

He hitched a thumb into his belt loop and cocked his head. "Well..."

"I don't blame you. Stranded in the middle of a hayfield?" She swung her legs out of the automobile and rose to her feet. But the near miss had taken its toll. Suddenly woozy, she staggered.

The hunk leaped forward, taking her arm, and supporting her. "Whoa! You sure you're okay?"

Olivia closed her eyes and bent slightly at the knees, allowing herself to be held. For the briefest of moments, she felt safe. When she straightened, her gaze met his yet again, and a tingly sensation zipped from her heart to her toes. But her early-warning defense system kicked in.

Mayday, mayday, it clamored. *Man, no good!*

Olivia ignored the warnings. This situation was unprecedented in her woefully limited experience.

"You're about the prettiest thing that ever sprouted up in this hayfield." The gent tipped his classic gray wool Stetson. "Hello. I'm Lance."

Seriously?

"Lance," Olivia breathed, only now becoming aware of the fact that she was still swooning in his arms.

This feels so good.

She giggled self-consciously and drew away from him. Never had she been in such a peculiar situation. But she was still unsteady on her feet, and she rested her broken psyche against the BMW's door frame. "I guess I'm a little dizzy, is all. For a minute there, I didn't think I was going to make it."

The brawny specimen, now identified as Lance, turned, and came to stand beside her. Resting his compact butt against the chassis, he said, "It was a narrow miss. I heard the horn and realized right away that you were in big trouble." He smacked his palms against the car frame. "This is a sweet machine. But no match for a semi, I'm afraid." Then he angled his head toward Olivia, looking at her hard. "You weren't texting, were you?"

"Oh, no. I wouldn't text and drive. I just…" She studied her hands, remembering them gripping the steering wheel as she tried to connect the chain of events that had landed her in this field. But her brain was a muddle. Olivia shrugged. "I lost my concentration for a second, and the next thing I knew, I was staring into the front grill of that monster truck."

And what the heck am I doing out here in a hayfield with freakin' Brad Pitt?

Lance massaged his temples and looked away. Then he turned back, his expression grave. "It happens. Out on the highway…no traffic to speak of…beautiful day…"

Olivia sighed, motioning toward the clipped bale of hay. "What a mess. I'm terribly sorry. I'll pay for the damages."

Lance waved a hand dismissively. "Forget it. It's nothing."

"Some kind of awful."

Lance leaned in and speared her with a pointed gaze. "You're one lucky girl."

Olivia raised her eyebrows. "I guess that's true. The Beemer's fine."

"More to the point, you weren't injured. Nor the dog, either." Lance eyed the car and grimaced. "But it's going to take some doing getting all that hay out of there."

"Ugh. And then some." Olivia shook her head, imagining the

onerous task that lay ahead. "But you know what?" she said brightly. "You're right. It could have been so much worse."

Lance gestured toward the guitar. "You play?"

"A little." Not wanting to brag, Olivia curled an amber lock of her shoulder-length hair around her index finger.

Lance crossed his impossibly long legs at the ankles and dug his heels into the soil. "Hmm...so, where are you headed if you don't mind my asking?"

Olivia hesitated. Where was she headed, and how much should she disclose to this stranger?

"Crystal Falls," she blurted. *Dang! Mouth not connected to brain.*

Lance cocked his head, eager for more details.

But suddenly Olivia was in no mood to oblige him. "I have business there," she said in a no-nonsense voice.

Lance swiped a hand across his dimpled jaw. "Just another two miles, and you'll be on the outskirts. You have family hereabouts?"

Olivia paused, still unsure how to respond.

"No," she finally said. "I don't know anyone from these parts...except you, that is." She extended a hand. "I'm Olivia, Olivia Barone."

"Oh, sorry. It's Crawford. Lance Crawford at your service, Ms. Barone." Lance shook her hand and then pushed off from the automobile, extending his arms wide. Proudly, he encompassed the panoramic countryside. "This is my family's spread."

"Friends call me Livy," Olivia said. "And she's a beauty...the farm that is."

Lance grinned. "She sure is, Livy." He eyed her appreciatively.

Olivia blushed. She knew he was teasing her, and it was a balm to her battered ego.

Then Lance's gaze fell upon the two-carat diamond ring encircling her finger, and his smile faded. "Don't mean to pry, Livy, but where's Mr. Barone?"

"Oh..." Olivia twisted the gemstone toward her palm away and out of sight. "No. It's not like that. I'm...not married. I...I was, but...he passed away."

The enormity of her lie instantly confounded her.

Lance looked momentarily stricken. "Forgive me. It's none of my business." He cleared his throat. "Ahem! Well, we'd better get you back on the highway, Livy. Where are you staying in Crystal Falls? I'll see to it you get there without further mishap." He turned and surveyed the shredded bale, the once-tidy field now strewn with hay, Olivia's formerly pristine-looking vehicle.

"At least I hope so."

Oliva was ashamed to admit that she had no plans. In fact, she had made no arrangements whatsoever. Suddenly, she realized she'd become a vagabond, a sketchy sort of person. "I'm...not sure." She glanced at the contents of her formerly white car. "I haven't decided where I'm staying. This was a spur-of-the-moment trip."

Lance's brows bunched. "I see," he said, obviously not seeing at all. "How long are you staying?"

Olivia looked away, suddenly unwilling to meet his eyes. "I don't know. I just thought I'd play it by ear. I may leave in a week. Or I might stay indefinitely." She turned back, feeling the warmth in her cheeks as her face reddened again. "I figured I'd wait and see how things panned out."

As if on cue, Milo barked, which offered her a welcome escape from his line of questioning.

"Milo," Olivia hollered. "Here!"

Sapped after his sprint around the field, Milo trotted over, his little pink tongue drooping from between narrow black lips.

"You scamp," she chastened him.

But Milo appeared totally unrepentant. He allowed himself to be scooped up in her arms and rewarded her with a doggie kiss to her nose.

Lance sighed audibly, and Olivia figured she'd been granted a pass. Surely, a dog lover would consider a dog person a good person and not some wayward vagrant.

Picking up as though they hadn't been interrupted, Lance said, "In that case, might I suggest Mrs. Bow's Charming Manor?"

At that, Olivia burst out laughing. Today would certainly count as the most bizarre day of her life.

"I know." Lance sucked on his teeth. "It's a bit over the top. I grant you. Most people hereabouts just refer to it as Charm or Mrs. Bow's."

"And does Mrs. Bow have a charming manner?" Olivia snickered.

Lance squared his shoulders and spoke in a measured tone. "She does, indeed. She's my paternal aunt and a wonderful woman. And mind you, she's particular. Auntie won't rent to just anyone off the street. The inn is chock-full of priceless antiques. But if she takes a fancy to you, she'll lease you a room for a week, a month, or in perpetuity. In fact, she very well might adopt you."

"Oh," Olivia exclaimed in a small voice. What was she getting herself into? Perhaps, at this point in her life, anonymity would be better than making lasting connections. She didn't know. Her befuddled brain was beginning to shut down. But one thing was for certain. She desperately needed a safe harbor. Perhaps Mrs. Bow's Charming Manor would prove the answer to her prayers.

Lance was intent on her, and she could feel his resolve weakening. Was he reconsidering, thinking perhaps that she was a liability risk? If he doubted his initial assessment, he did an excellent job of hiding it.

He bent to examine the car tires. Then, when he was satisfied that there were no punctures, turned back to Olivia. "You think this thing is safe to drive?"

Olivia nodded. "Yeah." She pressed the ignition, and the engine fired.

"Come on, then. Follow me." Lance whistled to his horse, and it trotted over to him. "First, we'll go back to my place." Taking hold of the reins, he fitted a booted toe into the left stirrup. In the moment before he mounted, Lance glanced back at Olivia and gave a nod of his head. "It'll take me fifteen minutes or so to get Guinevere unsaddled and into her stall, and then we'll be on our way."

Olivia raised an eyebrow, half a mind to disagree, but then she thought better of it. What were her alternatives? "Okey-dokey," she said, climbing into her car with Milo in tow.

Lance gave her a lopsided grin and then whistled for his dog. "Merlin!"

"Merlin? Guinevere?" Olivia muttered. "What have we stumbled onto here, Milo?"

Sitting up on his hind legs, the terrier put his front paws on her arm and yipped in reply.

"Camelot?" Olivia breathed, briefly meeting the dog's big brown eyes.

"Are you with me, Livy?" Lance called out before cantering off a short distance. Then he stopped and turned to her, waiting for her response.

"Yes." Olivia shifted to reverse. "I am intrigued."

"As am I," he said before galloping off.

Lance's last words were nearly inaudible. But Olivia heard them, and they gave her the slightest shred of hope. Hope that this strange exodus would turn out well.

It just has to.

Carefully, she maneuvered around the tattered hillock of hay. "Merlin," Olivia mouthed, shaking her head in disbelief. Then she shifted to drive and raised her left arm, signaling to her champion that all was well and that she was following.

"Lead on, fair knight," Olivia murmured, suddenly feeling as though a burden had been lifted. And then she found herself singing the *CAMELOT* theme song:

"It's true. It's true. The crown has made it clear. The climate must be perfect all the year. In Camelot."

TWO
BOW'S CHARMING MANOR

"Yes, Auntie Annabelle, we'll be there in two shakes." Lance held his cell phone before his chin while keeping an eye on the BMW in his rearview mirror. "She's lovely. Really. I haven't known her for very long, but she's a good person. One can just tell."

Up ahead, the traffic light turned from yellow to red, and he braked.

"What?" His voice rose shrilly. "A psychopath? Come on, Auntie. Have I ever let you down?"

Lance squirmed in his seat and then sat upright. "That's not fair," he complained, glancing about as if to assure there was no one else privy to this conversation. "I was nine years old, and that hell-cat of yours left a nasty scar on my otherwise perfect nose."

The light changed, and Lance laughed at something his aunt had said. Unhurriedly, he motored down an oak-lined thoroughfare, one that was abutted on either side by low stone walls bordering the deep plots situated beyond. He flicked on his left blinker and checked the mirror to assure himself that Olivia was following. Then he steered through stately black iron gates, up into a single-lane roadway canopied by massive red maples. The drive led to a sprawling Victorian gingerbread with clapboard walls painted a pale yellow and a wide front porch with white Doric-capped columns and oversized brass coach lanterns.

It was a Thomas Kinkaid painting come to life.

Lance peered at his nose in the rear-view mirror. "I know it makes me look dashing. Oh, never mind. We're in the drive now." He put the car in park, cut the ignition, and then thrust an arm out the driver's side window to motion for Olivia to pull up behind him. "She's here. You can judge for yourself, Auntie Annabelle."

Minutes later, Annabelle Bow stood at the front door, beaming. She was petite with an ample bosom that strained the confines of her bodice, and, despite the concerns she'd voiced only moments before, she radiated calm and good cheer.

"Lance, darling." She held out her arms, and Lance allowed himself to be swallowed up in them.

Lance disentangled himself from her embrace. "Auntie, I'd like you to meet my new friend, Olivia Barone." He turned toward the young woman hanging behind and then faced his aunt. "She's here on business. And she needs a place to stay. Naturally, I suggested Charm."

"Naturally." Annabelle eyed Olivia from head to toe. "How do you do, dear?"

"Very well. Thank you, ma'am."

Annabelle stared at the young woman, taking her measure. "Please, dear," she finally said. "Won't you indulge an old lady and take off those sunglasses?" The dowager wrinkled her nose. "The eyes, you know, the keyhole to the soul."

Olivia gulped, but there was nothing for it. Reluctantly, she complied, knowing full well that this small act might be her undoing. As she lifted the spectacles from off her face, she ducked her head. But in the next instant, Olivia stood tall. Let them think what they might, she thought, returning Annabelle's gaze. She hadn't done anything wrong.

Olivia could read their thoughts as they took in her black eye, their processing of the obvious, and despite her resolve, a feeling of humiliation washed over her. "It looks worse than it is. I'm…so clumsy," she prattled. "I walked right into a door, and—"

"Well, good heavens, come in, you two." Annabelle pointed her chin toward the horizon where the sun was slowly being swallowed. "Now that autumn has arrived, the days are shorter." She motioned them over the threshold. "It cools off quickly this time of day."

It hadn't taken long for Olivia to settle in at Mrs. Bow's Charming Manor. Lance had helped her move her things into one of Annabelle's guest suites. Then he'd insisted they exchange cell phone numbers, saying he'd check in on her tomorrow. Once he'd taken his leave, her first order of business had been to shower and wash the straw from her hair. Then she'd changed into a pair of slacks and a cotton sweater.

Now, at the request of her hostess, she was taking tea with her in Charm's sumptuous parlor and, much to her surprise, feeling quite at home. Before taking a sip, Olivia brought the wafer-thin, China teacup to her lips, breathing in the exotic aroma of cinnamon, vanilla, and chamomile. "Ahh," she sighed. The infusion warmed her insides, and the crackling fire in the gas fireplace did the same for her exterior.

"This is delightful, Annabelle," Olivia said. "The inn is beautiful. It was so kind of you—"

"My pleasure, dear. I confess, I like nice things, and I've been fortunate to have acquired some interesting pieces." The innkeeper's eyes darted about the lavishly appointed room.

"I'll say." Olivia patted the padded arm of her Bergère chair. "This fabric is gorgeous."

"Hand-screened chintz imported from France."

"And the furniture…you have such a collection of antiques." Olivia's eyes lingered on a secretary inlaid with rosewood that graced the wall opposite the fireplace.

Annabelle followed her gaze. "That piece is exceptionally fine, circa 18th century. I found it in Italy, 1970, while taking the grand tour."

"And you had the presence of mind to purchase it?" Olivia turned to her hostess, a look of incredulity on her face.

"I am an only child," Annabelle admitted.

"Me, too."

"Ah. Then perhaps you'll understand when I say I was a spoiled one."

"No." Olivia's face clouded. "That was not my experience but do go on."

Annabelle processed Olivia's words and then resumed. "My parents treated me to that holiday." She paused, momentarily lost in thought. "You see," she said, returning to the present. "I was to be married in the fall. To Raymond, the eldest Crawford brother."

"A Crawford?"

"Lance's uncle."

"I see." Olivia's brow knit at this revelation.

"Yes, very good-looking men in that family. Anyway, it was to be a special time for my mom and me to have one last mother-daughter adventure before I settled down with my soon-to-be husband."

"How nice," Olivia said, secretly wishing she'd had such an opportunity.

"Yes." Annabelle gestured toward the secretary. "We found that lovely thing in a tiny shop in Bologna, and we were both taken with it. My mother offered to buy it for me and have it shipped."

"Wow. Fortunate girl."

Annabelle cupped her chin in her hand and briefly stared out into space. Then she favored Olivia with a rueful half-smile. "Yes. I was very carefree and happy. But the marriage didn't last long."

"Oh? What happened?" Olivia gazed over the rim of her teacup, giving the matron her undivided attention.

"Raymond was killed in a boating accident just days before our first anniversary." Annabelle sighed.

"That's terrible!" Olivia gazed at Annabelle with eyes full of compassion. "I am so sorry."

The kindly innkeeper shrugged dismissively. "It's all ancient history. But I can't look at that piece without thinking of what might have been."

"Umm…" Olivia murmured. "We just never know. Do we?"

"No." Annabelle chuckled mirthlessly. "But I fell in love again."

"Well, good!"

"No. This time to a cad."

"Yikes." Olivia found herself hanging on Annabelle's every word. This woman was so open and considerate she couldn't help but feel empathy for her. "How so?"

Annabelle shook her head. "He was a philanderer, a real con man. And it didn't take him long to show his true colors. The honeymoon was barely over before I discovered him diddling his secretary."

"That's awful." Olivia straightened in her chair.

"As far as I know, he slept with every woman he ever employed."

"Yeow! What a rat."

"Yes, but I put up with his shenanigans for years. Foolish me. It wasn't until he had an affair with my best friend that I decided I'd had enough."

"You poor thing." Olivia frowned. She'd only known Annabelle for a short time, yet she felt a strong connection to her. "So, then what?"

"I've shied clear of men ever since," Annabelle said, matter-of-factly. "I decided it was better to be alone than to wish I were."

"Gosh. Well said." Olivia thought about her own predicament. How she had come to be here in Mrs. Bow's Charming Manor.

But Annabelle is lovely. She deserves a good man to adore her.

"Perhaps you should reconsider," she said. "You have so much to offer—"

Milo whimpered, and Annabelle and Olivia's eyes were instantly drawn to the small dog asleep at their feet. His little legs twitched as he dreamed a doggie dream.

"Most likely running after his new best friend," Olivia said, smiling at him indulgently.

"Oh?" Annabelle raised her brows.

"Lance's dog." Olivia bent at the waist and patted Milo's silvery head, and he quieted.

"Ahh. Merlin."

"That would be an affirmative."

Annabelle winked at Olivia, a small smile tugging at her lips. "Now, there's a real catch."

"Merlin?" Olivia feigned a look of skepticism.

"No, silly. His master, of course. Lance Crawford."

"He does seem awfully nice."

"Nice on the eyes, too."

"Oh, yeah. So, why's he still single?" Olivia tilted her head toward Annabelle, giving her a pointed look.

"Why else? He's been damaged. From what I understand, a woman broke his heart, and now he's afraid to give it away again."

"I see." Olivia didn't like where this conversation was leading. "Can't say as I blame him." It was time to change the subject and segue to more neutral ground. "Tell me more about these scrumptious furnishings."

Annabelle sipped the last of her tea and then placed her cup atop its saucer on the piecrust table between their two chairs. "Alright," she said, a faraway look in her eyes. "For a time, my father served as assistant to the ambassador to India."

"No kidding?"

"That's right. And many of the things you see here were collected by my parents while we were living abroad."

"How fascinating." Oliva gazed about the room with a new appreciation for its splendors.

"Of course, I was just a little girl. But I remember it as a magical time. It was as though we were leading enchanted lives."

"How so?" Olivia asked, intrigued.

Annabelle gazed into the fire as though mesmerized. Moments passed, and then she continued, "For one thing, we had servants. They did our every bidding, and for this, they were paid pennies."

Olivia's eyes grew round. "I don't understand. Why?"

"I know that sounds awful. But it's simply the way things were. At the time, I accepted it all at face value. It was, as I understand it, and still is a very unfair system."

"White privilege," Olivia muttered.

Annabelle grimaced. "Indeed. And caste. Such a horrible system."

"Mmhmm." Olivia nodded.

"Now that I've matured, gained some perspective, I have regrets. But I can't beat myself up over them. I simply wasn't evolved. Didn't consider the injustice of it."

"Interesting."

"We're all works in progress."

Olivia pondered. "I need to believe that."

"Do." Annabelle clapped her hands as if to dispel any negative energy. "Please, tell me, what brings you here to Crystal Falls and Mrs. Bow's? There are no coincidences in life. You realize that don't you, dear?"

"Uh…" Olivia faltered.

Do I dare tell all?

But Annabelle smiled at her with such compassion that Livy found herself confessing. "Truth be told, I had a wonderful yet terrible life. When it got so that the negatives outweighed the positives, I had to run…run away or risk losing myself."

Annabelle reflected for a moment and then spoke. "Is it possible to run away from one's troubles?"

"I don't know," Olivia answered. "I hope so."

"Tell me about him."

Olivia glanced at the clock atop the mantle. It was almost nine o'clock. She sighed, rested her head against the chair's back, and resolved to come clean. "I met him in my senior year in college. He was an ambitious young attorney, and moneyed. Ten years older than I, he was suave and sophisticated…"

The fire in the fireplace spat and crackled merrily. Licks of flame seemed to grow ever larger as shadowy figures danced in the blaze.

Olivia awoke to find herself alone in the room, a crocheted throw tucked around her. The fire had been reduced to glowing embers, and the mantle clock told her nearly four hours had elapsed since it had last been consulted. It was 12:30 a.m. Annabelle was nowhere to be seen, and her teacup had been replaced by a brandy snifter, empty but for dregs.

Olivia yawned and roused herself, only to have reality come crashing down upon her.

What am I doing here? Have I lost my mind?

At the sound of Annabelle's fluty voice, her feelings of despair retreated to the farthest corners of her cranium.

"Come on, little guy," the matron cried gaily, sweeping into the parlor with Milo trotting behind her.

Olivia straightened in her chair and pinned a smile to her face.

"Ah, you're awake, I see."

"Just barely. Forgive me. I must have dozed off."

"That you did." Annabelle stooped to pat Milo's grey head, and then she collected her brandy snifter and Olivia's teacup and saucer. "And it's no wonder after what you've been through."

Olivia shuddered inwardly. She was groggy, couldn't recall where she'd left off.

What gruesome details have I revealed?

But then Annabelle was cajoling her. "We're all locked up. So, it's off to bed with the two of you."

Olivia happily obliged; she unfolded herself from the chair and then padded up the stairs to her tastefully furnished bed chamber with Milo on her heels. The prospect of sleep. To lose herself in oblivion had never been more appealing.

THREE
THE LAY OF THE LAND

She'd been too weary to draw the drapes. Instead, she'd fallen into bed and slept the whole night through. It wasn't until almost nine o'clock when Olivia awoke the next morning, and if the sun hadn't been streaming directly into her eyes, she'd probably have slept even later. It took but a moment to get her bearings. When she did so, she sprang out of bed and dressed quickly. She didn't know why, but she felt different, lighter somehow. And then it came to her; the weight that had gradually settled like an anvil on her heart had lifted! A new day beckoned, and she was eager to get on with it.

After applying a bit of eye makeup and some concealer to the bruise beneath her eye, Olivia wandered downstairs only to find the place deserted. Eventually, she came upon a small glassed-in porch that served as Charm's breakfast room. There, she helped herself to a light meal of coffee and pastry, both of which had been thoughtfully provided on a sideboard. After eating, Oliva returned to her room to finish unpacking. Once her things had been stowed, she decided to explore.

"Come on, Milo," she said, lifting him off the bed. "It's time we got the lay of the land."

It was a glorious day, and Milo scampered about, off-leash, acquainting himself with Annabelle's rambling estate. Two hours later, after depositing him back in her room and filling his water-bowl, Olivia's stomach was rumbling, and she figured it was time to familiarize herself with the town of Crystal Falls and get something more substantial to eat.

In the bright sunlight, Main Street looked like an idealized village in a Hallmark made-for-TV movie. The Crystal Falls historic district was lined with a collection of painstakingly restored storefronts, all of which were doing a brisk trade. A tavern dating back to the turn of the century anchored the corner at the end of the block. High above its entry, a well-preserved sign proclaimed NESBITT'S in bold, black lettering. Below the script was a carved relief of a white-painted hand, several inches removed from an arm, to which it had—ostensibly—once been attached.

Inside and to the back, a polished, black walnut bar with intricate carvings and gleaming brass rails dominated the space. Flanking it were a phalanx of leather upholstered bar stools, nearly all of them occupied. And behind it, a dizzying array of red and amber-colored bottles. Wines, liquors, brews, as well as glasses of every size and configuration, lined the shelves. Despite the early hour, the saloon was hopping. Beneath the mullioned windows, all but one of the banquettes were occupied.

Lean and grizzled, a middle-aged man officiated over the bar while chatting up the few regulars who'd gathered for a quick lunch, an ice-cold draft, and the latest gossip. The county sheriff, easily identifiable in his drab, khaki green uniform emblazoned with a silver star badge, sat at the far end of the bar, nursing a mug of coffee. Although he sported a slight paunch, given his balding pate and robust frame, he cut a striking figure. A tall, gangly fellow clothed in a somber black suit, his face frozen in a permanent expression of affected sympathy, was seated on his right. One barstool removed was a stout chap of no more than five feet seven inches. Cherub-faced and chatty, it was obvious what this fellow lacked in height, he more than made up for in ardor. Rounding out the group were two tall drinks of water, who appeared to be cut from the same mold. They were rugged, tan, and sinewy with over large, callused hands that bespoke lifetimes of physical labor.

The thin, formally dressed man swiveled in his stool to address the uniformed officer. "It's a damned shame about Maggy Jenkins. Isn't that so, Chester?"

"Like you care, Les," the sheriff snorted. "Good thing she was rushed to the hospital. Soon enough she'll be just one more customer for you, eh? One more embalming job at Lowther's Funeral Parlor." He raised his right hand, sifting fingers over his thumb in the universal money sign, and laughed at his own poor joke. Then he turned to the sawed-off, compact fellow seated beside him. "Am I right, Timmy?"

Charlie stood behind the bar and grimaced.

"A little respect, Chester," Timmy chastised. "This is no laughing matter. With all that that woman's done for the kids in this town. Ask the Crawford brothers what they think, huh? As I recall, Lance was a student of hers." He shook his head and eyed the nearly identical pair. "Damn shame, I say."

"Oh, yeah." The taller of the two doppelgangers nodded. "I remember when Lance sang with the church choir. He was always a little Dennis the Menace, you know?" He elbowed his brother. "Remember, Rudy?"

"You got that right, Vince," Rudy agreed. "Forever up to some tomfoolery. I'm sure he drove Maggie crazy with his shenanigans, but she never complained, and he adored her."

"Hell, all the kids adore her," Timmy piped up. "The whole town loves her. She's an institution. And her annual Christmas pageant is, too."

"We'll all face the Grim Reaper at some time or another," Les said. "You just never know when your time is up."

"And you'll be ready to handle all the arrangements," Chester snickered.

"That's right," Timmy agreed. "So, drink up, fellows, and have another on me. Life is sweet but short. Here, here!" He raised his glass, and his companions followed suit. "To Maggy."

"To Maggy," the others chorused.

"So, what about the Christmas pageant?" Vince wiped his chin.

Les shook his head, looking even more doleful than usual. "Don't know. Canceled, I guess."

Chester recoiled as if struck. "No! It wouldn't be Christmas without the pageant. As sheriff, I have to say I think we should do everything in our power to see to it that the tradition continues." He gathered himself, preparing to orate. "Besides, it's a great little revenue generator. Times have been tough, and the local merchants need the business. We've just got to find someone to step in and direct the darn thing. That's all there is to it."

Charlie looked at Chester askance. "Yeah, sure. We need to do that, Chester. And who would you suggest?"

"I don't know. What about Bev Marfield? She plays piano pretty well, doesn't she? How hard can it be?"

Les sputtered, nearly spitting out his quaff. "Good Lord, Bev? She's a witch."

The others tittered, stared into their pints, and nodded.

"I'm sorry, fellows," Les said. "But you know it's true. Bev's mean as dirt. The kids wouldn't do diddly for her."

"Yeah." Vince warmed to the subject. "We've got to get someone with some...some pep. A person the kids will take a shine to."

Timmy snapped his fingers. "How about Kevin Grimes? Didn't he get a music degree from State? What about him?"

Charlie grimaced. "One, Kevin has the personality of a cement block. Two, I wouldn't trust him around my kids. That is, if I had any. He's so smarmy. There's something not right about him."

"No, no, not Kevin," Chester said. "I think he's harmless. But... I agree. Who then?"

At that moment, the front door swung open, and Olivia swept in. Wearing a crisp shirt-waist dress, her reddish-brown locks glossy from their recent washing, she was an attractive new face, and the men broke off their conversation and eyed her curiously.

Charlie palmed a menu and then darted from behind the bar. "Lunch for one, Miss?"

Olivia nodded. "Yes, thank you."

Charlie gestured. "Table? Or would a booth by the window suit you?"

"Booth, please."

Charlie led her to the empty booth, and Olivia slid in. Once seated, she glanced up at the bar to find five pairs of eyes fixated on her. Quickly, she averted her eyes. "What's up with them?" She pointed her chin toward the bar, and Charlie followed her gaze before turning back to her.

"Those guys?" He shrugged. "They're my mates, the local movers, and shakers. Friendly, I assure you, Today, they're in a huff because the director of our annual Christmas pageant is ill and unable to assume the reins this year."

"I'm sorry to hear that."

"Ah!" he exclaimed dismissively. "It's always something." He studied her face. "Haven't seen you around here, although you look awfully familiar."

"Olivia Barone," she said, extending a hand.

Charlie took it, gave it a brief shake, and released it.

"I'm from the Big Apple. I'm certain we've never met."

"Hmm…" The proprietor looked unconvinced, but he quickly recovered. "Charlie Nesbitt at your service."

Olivia's gaze darted about the room, and then she smiled at her host. His salt and pepper gray hair was neatly trimmed, and his penetrating dark eyes were creased at the corners. She pegged him at late forties, early fifties, a pleasant-looking fellow. "Nice place. Is it yours?"

"Yes, indeed." Charlie peered at her.

Olivia put two fingers to her cheek. "What is it?" she asked, suddenly uncomfortable and shifting in her seat.

"Nothing." Charlie shook his head as if to clear it. He handed her a menu. "Today's specials are there on the right-hand column. Soup, today, is bean. It's fresh and powerful."

Olivia laughed and shook her head. "No powerful soup for me, sir." Briefly, she perused the menu. "How are your burgers?"

"A-number-one," Charlie said. "And how would you like that cooked?"

"Medium rare with the works?"

"Highly recommended."

Olivia passed the menu back to Charlie.

"You won't be disappointed." The trim restaurateur stepped away from the table.

"And a Coke, please."

"Coming right up, sweetheart." Charlie smiled at her and turned to go.

Olivia snorted, a barely concealed chuckle, and Charlie whirled back to face her. "What's the joke? I could use a laugh."

"I'm sorry," Olivia said. "That was rude of me. It's just that…"

Charlie folded his arms and cocked his head, inviting her to continue. "Yes?"

Olivia reddened. "Uh…it's just that…in the city…I would have taken offense at the…well…at the 'sweetheart,' if you must know."

"Is that so?" Charlie raised his eyebrows, looking perplexed.

Olivia nodded an affirmative. "Yes. But here, in Crystal Falls, I find that I'm fine with it. I was laughing at myself, you see. Because my typical reaction would be to bristle at that word. Somehow in this place, the *sweetheart* just seems genuine and right."

"True on both accounts," Charlie said. "You city broads can have a pretty tough veneer. At least that's been my experience. And don't get me wrong. That's okay. It's a necessary defense mechanism. I get it. But here in our little town? You won't much be needing it."

"I'm beginning to realize that."

Charlie clicked his tongue by way of answer. Then he set off toward the kitchen.

"Burger, bloody, dressed, with fries," he barked to the kitchen as he rounded the bar, and Olivia stifled giggles.

"Bloody dressed?" she murmured under her breath. "What a character!"

Once he'd gone, she withdrew a compact and a tube of concealer from her purse. Opening the compact, she regarded her reflection in the tiny mirror. "Just a bit more coverup," she murmured. After a quick look around to make sure no one was watching, she dabbed concealer on the bruise beneath her eye.

As soon as Charlie returned to his place behind the bar, the local newsmongers leaned in toward him, eager for details and fodder for gossip. But he ignored them; he picked up a rag from the sink and swiped at a nonexistent spot on the bar countertop.

"So, who is she, Charlie?" Lester breathed.

Charlie shrugged but didn't look up. "Damned if I know."

"Pretty girl," Timmy said. "She's a looker, alright!"

"Wonder what she's doing here." Furtively, Chester eyed the young woman seated at the booth.

"A fellow wouldn't forget a face like that," Timmy said. "In fact…" He looked up and to the side while searching his memory bank.

"What?" Charlie's raspy voice brought the stocky landowner out of his reverie.

"There's something about her," Timmy said. "I'm sure I've seen her somewhere before."

Vince landed a playful punch on Rudy's shoulder. "I bet she's the gal Lance was jabbering on about."

"What are you talking about?" Charlie asked, peering at the Crawford brothers.

"Fool woman lost control of her vehicle," Vince explained. "Went flying off the highway and nearly flipped her car in our hayfield."

"That's right," Rudy agreed. "Hell of a mess. Hay ever'where!"

"If it is her, I can tell you she's staying at the Charm with Annabelle," Vince added.

"Bow's, huh?" Les cupped his chin in hand. "The chick must have money, eh?"

"Alright, alright, enough about the damn girl," Chester said, a note of desperation creeping into his voice. "Who're we gonna get to direct the pageant?"

The men looked at one another, but no one spoke. They shook their heads balefully, pondering his question.

Olivia was plucking a few bills from her wallet when Charlie appeared at her table. "There's a tip in there for you, sir." Olivia placed the money on the table and grinned at the proprietor.

"Thank you kindly." Charlie reached out to help her from the booth.

"How was the burger?"

"Wonderful." Oliva rose to her feet. "Best burger I've had, well, since forever."

Charlie hooted. "You were just hungry, sweetheart. But I'd say that was a compliment coming from a cosmopolitan girl like yourself."

"And you would be correct." Olivia allowed herself to be escorted to the front door. "I'm thinking of staying here awhile. So, you'll probably see me again."

"Fine by me. You add a touch of class to the joint." Charlie let go of her elbow, opened the door, and held it for her. "Don't be a stranger."

Olivia stood on the threshold, hesitating. Suddenly, without warning, she whirled around and faced the bar. As expected, all eyes at the end of it were, once again, upon her. "Gentlemen?" She took in the tall, gangly fellow, the short, pudgy guy, a John Wayne imposter, and two good-looking, weather-buffed, middle-aged gents, who were so alike they might have been twins.

They stared back at her, their faces wearing innocent expressions, and Olivia chuckled inwardly for having had the chutzpa to call them out. "Good afternoon."

"Good afternoon, Miss," the assembled townsmen chorused.

Olivia tilted her head, suddenly feeling playful and enjoying the drama. "And by the way…"

The men leaned toward her, raptly holding on to her words.

"I'll have you know I'm a darned good musician and great with kids." Then Oliva turned back to Charlie and grinned at him impishly. "Yeah. I'll be around. You can bet on it."

"Right-o," Charlie chortled, admiring her spunk. "Be seeing you, sweetheart."

Olivia strolled down the sidewalk, a new look of confidence on her face. There was something about this place. She felt comfortable here, as though she could let her guard down and just be herself. But when a heavy hand clamped on her shoulder, her ebullience evaporated. Had Eric found her already? Olivia froze, preparing for the worst.

"Hey lady, where are you off to in such a hurry?"

At Lance's now-familiar voice, Olivia's shoulders sagged, and she put a hand to her chest. "Lance, you startled me." She turned to face him, laughing in relief. "You scared the hell out of me."

"I didn't mean to."

"You're not following me, are you?" she teased.

Looking taken aback, Lance shook his head.

"You're not some sort of stalker?"

But now, Lance was on to her and having none of it. He understood her game. "Guilty as charged."

Olivia's eyebrows shot up at his answer.

"It's true," Lance admitted. "My dad called me at the office, said he'd seen you at Nesbitt's."

Olivia nodded, but her expression said she was not really following.

Lance gestured. "My office is just around the corner. When I heard that you were here, so near at hand, I hightailed it out of there." He snapped his fingers. "And here I am."

Olivia smiled, and, without giving it any thought, linked arms with him. Lance acted as if that were the most natural thing in the world, and the two resumed walking, this time side-by-side.

Olivia chuckled, and Lance inclined his head. "What's so funny?"

"I swear. Men are bigger gossips than women."

Lance shrugged a grudging affirmative.

Olivia dug an elbow into his side. "Which one was your dad?"

"The good-looking one," he said. "Acorn doesn't fall far from the tree, you know."

"Well, there were two of them. Looked like twins. Could hardly tell them apart."

Lance nodded. "Dad's the taller of the two. The other guy is my Uncle Rudy."

"I guess they grow them big around these parts." Olivia shot him an appraising look. "Good genes in your family."

"Yep." Lance agreed. "Big guys, big hands, big feet..." He caught her eye and grinned wickedly.

"I get your drift," Olivia snickered. "Big heart?"

Lance affected a choirboy's innocence. "That, too."

"Umm. Everyone's friendly around here. It's weird."

"No," Lance said. "It's normal. Crystal Falls is a close-knit little town." He motioned toward the village, its main thoroughfare beckoning with attractive, well-appointed shops distinguished by tastefully painted signage, then to the hills bunched beyond, with their tracery of blackened tree branches lacing the sky. "We're not pretentious. We don't put on airs."

"It's refreshing."

"Here in Crystal Falls, what we do is pull together. We look after one another."

"You were looking out for me?"

Lance stopped walking and faced Olivia, searching her eyes, and Olivia felt as though she was drowning in his.

In the next moment, Olivia's cell phone jangled, and the spell was broken. "Darn it," she muttered, glancing at her cell's display. "Don't worry. It's a spam call."

"Go ahead and take it," Lance said. "I can wait."

"No. It's not important." Olivia pocketed her cell and focused on the intriguing man at her side. "Where were we?"

Lance squared his shoulders. "I...I was just wondering..." he stammered.

"About?" Olivia arched a brow.

"If I could take you out."

"Out?" Once again, Olivia was enjoying his discomfort. Teasing him was fun. "Out where?"

Lance drove his thumbs into his belt loops. Olivia could tell by the smile curling his lips that he knew he was being given the business. An unspoken message glinted in his eyes saying that, truth be told, he didn't half care.

"To dinner," he said, smoothly.

But Olivia could tell by the tone of his voice, he had more than a meal on his mind. Unless, that is, she was to be the main course. "Ugh." She patted her flat tummy. "I'm so full; I can't even think about food."

"Had the burger, huh?" Lance snickered. "It'll fill you up, all right. But I can guarantee that you'll be ready to eat again by about seven tomorrow evening."

"Jeez, Louise," Olivia muttered. "Does everyone around here know everybody else's business?"

"Yeah, pretty much." Lance nodded. "That's why we're all curious about you, missy."

Oliva drew back. "Aha. So, you thought you'd take me out, ply me with food and drink, and then grill me, huh?"

"Ah, you're on to me." Lance feigned a look of remorse.

"Hmm...I don't know. Can I trust you?" Olivia struggled to keep a straight face.

"It's just dinner..." Lance drew away, affecting an aggrieved expression. "What? You think I'm some hayseed living in this backwater and not worth your time?"

"Not at all." Olivia shot back. She realized she'd struck a chord, and now she wanted only to return to their easy banter. "Far from it." She looked him up and down and then widened her eyes. "I actually think you're terribly urbane."

Lance snorted. "Let's not overdo it." He exhaled, shoved his hands in his pockets and took a step away from her. "Look, I know you're a class act, and you probably think I'm beneath you. I may have been raised on a farm, but I'm an attorney and a damned good one. I've got a law degree from Harvard hanging on my office wall, and there's an Esquire after my name. I imagine I can keep up with the likes of you."

"Honestly, that has nothing to do with it," Olivia said, her expression suddenly grave. She'd been hurt. Annabelle said that Lance had been, too. He'd been kind to her, and she certainly didn't want to add to his problems. She chose her next words carefully. "I find you...*very* attractive. It's just that I'm...well...I don't know that I'm ready to—"

"Eat dinner?" Lance interrupted.

"Good heavens!" Olivia raised her arms and then let them fall helplessly to her side. "I can't say I've ever had a more compelling invitation."

Lance bent down and brought his face level with hers. "Well, then..."

Try as she might, Olivia couldn't help but laugh at his dogged persistence. "Okay," she said. "I accept. What time?"

Lance rose to his full height, which was considerable. "Pick you up at six-thirty."

"By which time I'll be ravenous." Olivia grinned indulgently.

Lance's face split in a self-satisfied smile, and Olivia breathed a sigh of relief. They were back on sure footing.

For some reason, she found that comforting.

FOUR
SEARCHING

The next morning, Olivia stood on the sidewalk gazing up at the Crystal Falls County Courthouse. With its red brick walls, white-painted trim, and fluted columns, it was a grand Georgian edifice. Once inside, however, she found that, like so many Federal buildings of its era, the interior had been reduced to a warren of narrow corridors and bland open spaces, a confusing maze, which she set out to explore. After a few dead ends, Olivia finally stumbled upon her destination, the County Records Repository.

Now, she leaned against a counter in a drab, windowless room behind which was housed, presumably, the object of her mission. She rang the bell on the countertop, and almost immediately, an attractive black woman darted out from the back room. She appeared to be in her early forties and very fit, obviously having logged long hours in the gym.

"Hello there. I thought I knew every soul in Crystal Falls," she said. "You're not from around here, are you?"

"No. But I think I might have a connection."

The woman's face clouded, and Olivia realized she was being obtuse and babbling. "You see, that's why I'm here."

The woman stared at Olivia. "You don't say?"

Get a grip.

Olivia extended her right hand. "I'm Olivia Barone."

The woman took Olivia's hand in hers. "Celia Hawthorne," she said. "Pleased to meet you."

"My friends call me Livy."

"Cee Cee."

The two smiled tentatively at one another.

"How can I help you?" Celia asked.

"I was hoping to examine your birth records from the year 1983."

"Birth records," Celia exclaimed. "My goodness! I haven't been asked to produce anything like that in..." She raised her brows, considering. "Well, in fifteen years or more, I guess."

Olivia's face fell. "I was afraid of that."

"What are you looking for, anyway?"

Olivia glanced first to the left and then to the right, as though reassuring herself no one was within earshot. Then, in an aside, she whispered, "It's personal."

"Oh." Celia digested this bit of news. "Forgive me. I didn't mean to pry."

"Not at all." Olivia shook her head. "Cee Cee, I'll be honest. I'm trying to locate my birth father. So far, all I've managed to come up with is that he might be from around these parts."

At this information, the clerk's eyes grew round. "I hate to disappoint you, Livy, but births are not recorded here. We've got recordings of death certificates, and you could research property owners. But we don't have recordings of birth certificates."

"Really?" Olivia cocked her head. "Then how does one go about researching birth certificates?"

"Girl," Celia said, tapping the countertop with a manicured fingernail. "Online, of course. You can get records of just about anything online. You might have to pay a modest fee, but that's the way to go. I thought everyone knew that."

"Well, darn." Olivia screwed up her face. "I guess I've been a bit out of the loop. Now, you're making me feel ancient as well as foolish."

"That certainly wasn't my intention, Livy." Celia grinned. "Do you have access to a computer? Because if you don't, I can set you up with one."

"I've got a laptop at home…that is at Charm, where I'm staying."

"Mrs. Bow's, huh? Nice digs," Celia said.

"Very. I feel like I died and went to heaven."

"I'd love to see the inside of that place."

"In that case, you must stop by one day, and I'll give you the tour."

"Cool. I'll take you up on that offer. But back to the matter at hand. You need to go to the Vital Records National Registry site, or just google 'birth records Crystal Falls County', and all kinds of sites will pop up." She scribbled the address on a post-it.

Olivia breathed a sigh of relief. "Thanks, Cee-Cee," she said. "You're a doll."

"I know." Celia waggled her eyebrows and then made a shooing motion. "You be sure to come back and tell me how you make out."

"I will," Olivia said. "You can bet on it, and then we'll arrange for that tour."

Two hundred and forty-five miles to the south, Eric Barone paused before the door to his office. Darkly handsome, but for deep set eyes that seldom smiled, he was impeccably attired in a hand-tailored suit of the finest wool. Briefly, he considered the etched lettering on the frosted-glass pane proclaiming DISTRICT ATTOR-NEY, and bile rose to his throat. The title gave him no satisfaction. He should have won the election! A judgeship was what he'd been destined for, a position that implied gravitas and one for which he was infinitely more suited. What really rankled was that he'd lost the election by less than two hundred votes.

He wrenched the door open, and it scraped against the side of his highly polished Gucci Horsebit Leather shoe, leaving an unsightly scuff. "Damn it!" Eric's fingers scrabbled across his cheek, seeking out the newly scabbed furrows she'd left there.

That bitch had made a mess of his once orderly life!

He let the door slam shut behind him, vainly hoping to erase the image of their last violent encounter. But it was no use.

It had been her fault, as usual. She'd pushed him over the brink, and he'd lost it. Eric paced in front of his sleek, steel, and maple-veneered desk. Agitated, he tugged his phone from his back pocket.

"Sanctimonious little wench," he muttered. "Leave me, will you?" Eric cleared his throat. "Hey Siri," he barked. "Call Olivia Barone."

It didn't surprise Eric when Olivia's cell immediately rolled over to voicemail. "You can't run from me forever, Livy," he spat into his phone. "I'll find you. You know I will. And when I do… well, let's just say you ain't seen nothin' yet."

Eric took a deep breath, struggling to get his smoldering rage under control. His eyes cut to a framed photo of Olivia on his desk. He picked it up and held it close to his face and, despite himself, he couldn't help but admire her lovely face, her perfect hourglass body. He willed himself to affect a less abrasive tone. He plunked down in his desk chair. "Listen, Liv. You've been a very bad girl. But…I'll admit, I'm partly to blame."

"I'm sorry," he said, "There. Are you happy? I said it. So, let's put this all behind us. I'm willing to meet you halfway."

Eric swiveled in his chair, warming to this tactic. "Come back home, and I'll make it up to you." His voice caught in his throat at the thought. "I promise."

But that was all he could manage. It was too much emotion, and he tamped it down, pushing away from this unfamiliar and prickly feeling. Eric swiped to disconnect, ending the call, and his vile humor resurfaced.

"Damn it!"

He was preparing to rise from his desk when his cell rang. Eagerly, Eric snatched up the phone, but one glance at the display, and he slumped back in his chair. "Hello? Oh, it's you." He sighed. "Hey, Brad."

He swiveled in his executive chair. Back and forth, back and forth. But rather than calming him, this rocking motion only made him all the more agitated.

"No!" His voice rose shrilly, and he planted his feet on his worsted wool carpet. "I haven't heard a word from her! It's been three days now. I'm beside myself." He listened to the voice on the line and then snapped, "I *know* we're expected to make an appearance! You'll just have to offer an excuse. She's ill. She has the flu. What can I say?" Eric dug a finger into his scalp, boring a hole in the thick black hair above his right ear. "So sorry my wife's run away?" He held the phone to his ear, nodding in agreement. But then something Brad said set him off again, and he bounded to his feet.

"Don't patronize me," Eric roared, fully incensed. "Of course, I'll be there." He resumed pacing. "Yes, I'll make nice. Now you listen to me. Have you had any luck tracking her cell phone? Well, why not? Get on it. And keep the pressure on at headquarters. She's missing. Her car could be in a ditch somewhere. Anything could have happened."

He listened to the voice on the speaker and then said. "You know it, and I know it, but no one else does. I want her back. You hear me? And I don't care how. There are ways…" Once again, he cast his eyes on the photo of Olivia. "Yeah, yeah, I'll be careful. You too, buddy." Eric ended the call, replaced the framed photo, and then dropped the phone on his desk.

"Oh, I'll make it up to you, Livy," he growled. "You'll see. In ways, you never dreamed of."

The suite Mrs. Bow had assigned to Olivia was a welcoming haven of serenity and refined elegance. The walls had been painted a deep rose, and the room was dominated by a mahogany poster bed piled high with white, lace-trimmed linens and down-filled pillows. Milo lay curled on his own bed set atop the coverlet, snoring softly. Olivia was seated before the mirror attached to a Louis XV-style, antique vanity, willing herself to relax before her date. Then her cell phone chimed.

She eyed the display. As feared, it was Eric, and her heart plummeted. Rather than accept the call, she hurled the phone across the room only to have it land on the bed. Awakening with a start, Milo barked hysterically.

"Milo, stop it," Olivia cried, and the little terrier soon quieted and settled back down again. Olivia propped her elbows on the vanity and held her head in her hands. Her life was a disaster.

A knock on the door brought her back to the present, and Olivia squared her shoulders. After casting a cursory glance at her reflection in the mirror, she crossed to the door and opened it.

Annabelle stood on the threshold, her open face radiating good cheer. But one look at the distraught young woman, and the kind-hearted innkeeper's smile vanished. "Olivia...what's the matter, child? You look as though you've seen a ghost." Annabelle didn't wait to be invited in but came to stand before Olivia.

"Worse. He keeps calling. He'll find me."

"That's impossible."

Olivia chuckled humorlessly. "You don't know him. Once Eric sets his mind to something, he doesn't let up. He's probably tracked me down already." She surveyed the room, determining how quickly she could pack and flee. "I have to leave."

"Don't go getting paranoid on me," Annabelle cautioned. "You're perfectly safe here, and you don't have to go anywhere you don't want to. Besides, Lance is waiting for you downstairs. Take my advice; put the whole thing out of your mind. Go have a little fun, why don't you? It just might do you a world of good."

Annabelle rested her palms on Olivia's shoulders and looked deeply into her eyes. "Trust me on this. It's going to be okay."

Olivia considered and then, despite the whirlwind addling her brain, nodded.

"Thata girl. I'll tell that nephew of mine you'll be down in a minute. And don't worry about the dog." In one fluid motion, Annabelle collected Milo from the bed. "We've bonded. Haven't we, little guy?" Milo's only response was to lick her chin. "I've grown attached to this furball. He can keep me company while you're out on the town."

FIVE
THAT RASCAL RHETT

Charming Manor's main stairway led down to an open hall off the parlor. Dressed in a classic trench coat over a fluttery, silk skirt and a lightweight sweater, Olivia skipped down those stairs displaying no sign of her earlier misgivings. With every step she descended, her mood lightened. So, by the time she met Lance, who was waiting for her below, she felt as unburdened and carefree as a butterfly.

At the sight of her, Lance's eyes lit up, and he whistled a low catcall. "Don't you look nice?"

"Why, thank you, sir." Olivia grinned, allowing her eyes to roam up and down Lance's muscular frame. It was plain to see he'd taken pains with his dress. He was wearing a preppy, navy crewneck sweater over a crisply pressed, checked oxford shirt, winter weight tan khakis, and a woolen, camel-colored overcoat. He looked like a Ralph Lauren ad fresh from the pages of GQ. "You clean up pretty well yourself."

Lance opened the front door, and Olivia sashayed before him, fastening the belt on her canvas coat as she did so.

Once inside Lance's Range Rover, Olivia hunched her shoulders and rubbed her hands together. "Brr! I should have worn gloves."

"Yeah. A cold front's coming in." Lance reached in front of her and opened the glove compartment. "Take these."

"What?"

"Gloves, silly." He handed her a pair of tan, calfskin mitts. "The temperature's dropping like a rock. We may even get snow. Say goodbye to Indian summer."

Olivia pulled the too-large leather gloves on her small hands. "Ooo, that *is* better." She waggled her fingers, and the empty fingertips flapped. "So, where are you taking me?"

"You'll never guess."

"Oh, dear."

Fifteen minutes later, Lance pulled into a parking lot over-flowing with pickup trucks and SUVs.

"BPOE Hall?" Olivia looked at him askance and chuckled.

Lance slotted the Rover into the last available space.

"I take you to the best places," he said with a sly side-smile.

Inside, the large hall was bustling with activity. In the entryway, Olivia shucked off the oversized gloves and shrugged out of her coat while gazing intently around. The women attired in brightly colored dresses, the men in sweaters and chinos, children of all ages dashing about, the lot of them chatting, laughing, and reveling in the camaraderie. "You were right; this is not what I expected."

"By that, you mean candlelight and a good bottle of wine?"

"Something like."

"Just trying to keep you on your toes. Besides, I thought you might enjoy meeting a few of the townsfolk."

"Sure. This looks like fun."

"Listen. We don't have to stay long, but it's good to make an appearance. You see, once a year, the whole town turns out for this function to benefit the Samaritan Center. It's for a good cause. Of course, I'd be happy to take you someplace a bit more elegant—"

"No, no." Olivia cut him off. "This is great. It's so...homey." She put her nose in the air. "And the food smells divine."

"Well then, let me have those." But before Lance could collect her things, the sheriff had swooped in, eager to make an impression.

He bowed slightly. "Chester Parker. How do?" he asked, nodding toward Lance.

"Sheriff," Lance said. "I believe you've met Olivia."

"Not officially." Chester took Olivia's hand in his. "But I've seen her, alright."

"Hello, Sheriff," Olivia dimpled.

"And I hear she's a damned good musician." Chester raised his brows and nodded, and then he was off to meet and greet some other potential voter.

"What was that all about?" Lance asked. But before Olivia could answer, the gangly funeral director, Les Lowther, and his stout sidekick, Timmy Corker, were beside them.

"Good evening, Lance," Les intoned in his dolorous voice.

"Evening," Lance said. Then he turned toward Olivia. "May I present Olivia Barone? She's here visiting."

"Hey there." Timmy Corker glanced at Lance and then turned to Olivia. "I hope you're finding Crystal Falls to your liking." He shook her hand exuberantly.

"Oh, yes," Olivia gushed, awkwardly disentangling her slender fingers from his chubby ones. "Everyone is so friendly. I feel right at home."

"Ever been here before?"

"Can't say that I've had the pleasure." Olivia arched a brow. "Why do you ask?"

"Just curious. And you're here because…?" Timmy asked.

"Family business."

Lance frowned. "Say, what's with the third degree?"

"That's not the way it is." Timmy hastened to cover his tracks. "It's just not every day we have the pleasure of welcoming a lovely young lady to our fair city."

"It's all good," Les barged in. "Family's good. Perhaps you could be persuaded to extend your stay, Ms. Barone."

"Yes," Timmy said. "Word is, you're a fine musician and great with kids."

Lance furrowed his brow and peered at Olivia, a question on his face.

Olivia bit her lip in an effort to contain her laughter. "True on both accounts, gentlemen. Suddenly, I'm parched." She looked to

Lance, then smiled brightly at the two other men. "Won't you excuse us?"

Lance took Olivia's elbow and steered her away, but Timmy's eyes followed the pretty newcomer. "I swear," he muttered, "I've seen that woman before."

"That was weird," Lance said under his breath.

"Not really," Olivia soothed. "I'm the new girl." She lowered her voice conspiratorially for a moment. "An enigma. They just want to figure me out. Say, why don't you stash those things and meet me at the drinks table?" She handed him his gloves and her coat.

Lance bowed slightly before ducking into the cloakroom, which opened to the left of the vestibule. In his absence, Olivia took a step into the main hall and paused to look around. The long tables had been covered in white paper cloths, and each one boasted an arrangement of autumnal blooms. Across the large space, she spotted Lance's kin, Vince and Rudy Crawford. The tall, ruggedly handsome pair were chatting up a middle-aged couple. Next to them, she spied Charlie Nesbitt. He caught her eye and raised a palm, and she returned his silent greeting. And, in between, a multitude of children, from reeling toddlers to gawky adolescents, darted about, all of them dressed in their Sunday finest.

In the next instant, the refrain of a familiar melody filled the air; it was the same arrangement of MY COUNTRY 'TIS OF THEE she'd heard on the radio just before her near collision, and she looked about, eager to find its source. It took but a moment for her to locate the bandstand from where a sandy-haired, burly fellow was strumming an enormous Fender Stratocaster guitar.

As always, the music enticed her. Even as a little girl, her mother had forever been afraid of losing her if live music were playing somewhere, for she knew from experience that Olivia would wander off to find its source. So, it was no surprise when Olivia found herself in front of the bandstand next to a card table displaying CDs and sheet music.

She gaped up at the musician. "Hi," she cried, waving an arm like a giddy fan.

"Hey, Rhett," Lance cried, charged in and running interference.

"Hello, yourself." Rhett's eyes roved over Olivia's shapely figure.

Lance turned to Olivia. "There you are. I thought I'd lost you. Weren't we supposed to meet at the drinks table? I got you a white wine." He handed off the drink, and Olivia accepted it gladly.

Rhett leaned over the guitar, grinning widely. "Where did you find this gorgeous creature?"

"You wouldn't believe me if I told you."

"Oh, yeah? Try me."

"In the middle of our hayfield."

Embarrassed, Olivia ducked her head and drank deeply.

"You're right," Rhett said. "I never would have come up with that one. Aren't you the lucky fellow?"

"Rhett," Lance said, smiling tightly. "Allow me to introduce Olivia Barone."

Rather than answer, Rhett strummed his guitar and improvised, his full-throated baritone resonating as he sang:

"I once met a girl,
Olivia.
Who excelled at pursuits great and
Trivial.
She was lovely and fine,
Like a rose off the vine,
And I found her both sweet,
And convivial.
Olivia, Livy lay ah.
Won't you come and live with me?
Say yah!
Olivia, Livy lay ah.
How happy we two,
Shall be, Livy.
For now, that I've seen thee,
I yearn for ye keenly.
Olivia, Livy lay,
Ah, Livy Livy!

And, Livy, I'll stay,
With you, yah!"

Rhett laughed uproariously, and Olivia blushed, while it was all Lance could do to maintain his composure and keep a stiff smile on his face.

"I can't believe this. Yours was the first voice I heard in Crystal Falls," Olivia babbled. "I heard you on the radio on my way into town."

"Keep it tuned to 1370 on your AM dial, where I'm keeping it real for you," Rhett's polished radio voice boomed. He waved a hand in the direction of DJ equipment, headphones, midi controller two-deck console, set out on a card table behind him.

Lance's eyebrows lowered. Rhett was openly flirting with his date. "Okay then." He tapped Olivia's shoulder. "I heard tell someone's starving, poor thing." Bodily, he put himself between Rhett and Olivia. "What say we get a bite to eat?"

Pretending not to notice Lance's irritation, Olivia turned and thumbed through a copy of Rhett's songbook. She hummed to herself as she sight-read the music. "This is great stuff. You're very talented, Rhett."

"Why, thank you, ma'am. Do you play?"

The double entendre was obvious in the musician's extended drawl and matching leer, and Lance's face darkened at this line of questioning. But Olivia merely shrugged her shoulders, enjoying the trivial banter. It had been far too long since she'd felt desirable, and she was reveling in the attention of these two handsome men.

"Piano, guitar...bassoon," she trilled, playfully.

"Ah, tonguing. Maybe we could do something together, huh?" Rhett asked. "How's about a little jam session some time?"

"Love it."

"Come on, Livy," Lance pressed a palm to the small of Olivia's back, and he steered her away from the bandstand. "We'd better get in line before the food's all gone."

"Bye-bye," Rhett called after them, his voice syrupy.

As she was being led away, Olivia craned her neck and smiled back at Rhett.

In turn, he sang her a farewell.

> "Olivia, Livy lay,
> Ah, Livy Livy!
> And, Livy, I'll stay,
> With you, yeah!"

Olivia and Lance made their way to the far side of the room where the buffet table was set, and Rhett segued into one of his original compositions.

"I never could stand that showoff," Lance complained.

"I'm sure he's harmless," Olivia countered.

"Don't be so sure."

At the buffet, they came upon the Crawford brothers and the couple Olivia had spied them speaking with earlier.

"Hi, Dad, Uncle Rudy," Lance called out.

The brothers turned to them simultaneously and smiled. "Son," Vince said. "And you must be Olivia." The taller of the two thrust out a hand, and Olivia took it.

"How do you do, sir?"

"So, this is the little lady who created such havoc in our hayfield, huh?" Vince teased.

Olivia grimaced. "I am *so* sorry! I offered to pay—"

Vince raised a palm, cutting her off. "No, no. It's nothing. We wouldn't hear of it."

"Don't mind him." Rudy grinned, instantly putting Olivia at ease. "He's just trying to get a rise out of you."

"Are you all settled in at my sister-in-law's place?" Vince asked solicitously.

"Yes, it's divine," Olivia said. "And Annabelle's a dear."

"That she is," Rudy agreed. "She's a fine woman."

"And where are the Misses Crawford?" Olivia asked.

At that, Rudy and Vince looked uncomfortable, and Olivia immediately regretted her question.

"I apologize," Lance said. "I should have told you. My mother passed away when I was just a boy." He gestured toward his uncle. "Uncle Rudy is the town's confirmed bachelor. So, as you can see, I grew up in a houseful of men."

"Oh, my," Olivia murmured.

"Don't be alarmed. Annabelle has kept us civilized."

"Well, it seems she's done a good job of it," Olivia said.

They edged toward the front of the line and began filling their plates. "Oh, they have pasta salad!" Olivia eyed the pretty crystal serving bowl filled with short twisty noodles, red bits of tomato, and shiny green basil leaves.

"Yes, with feta cheese and sundried tomatoes. That's one of Jane Gennarelli's specialties. Good cooks in Crystal Falls." Rudy helped himself and then offered her the serving spoon. "You'd best try some."

"And you'll want some of Anne Alexander's parmesan salmon," Lance said, depositing a forkful on her plate. "It's a standout. No buffet is complete without this splendid dish."

"Umm…yummy!" Olivia said. "And it's all so inviting!"

"Wait till you taste it," Vince said. "But do save room for some of Amy Schade's homemade cookies." He pointed his nose toward the end of the table where individual servings of decadent-looking deserts were dished out onto small paper plates.

"Gosh, this is fabulous," Olivia gushed. Then she leaned into Lance and said in a low voice, "Yep, I'd say Annabelle did a good job taming you Crawford men."

As they neared the end of the line, Vince gestured toward the couple ahead of them. "Say, have you met the Olsons?"

The pair turned and smiled at them, acknowledging the introduction.

"You've probably run into them. They're staying at Charm, too."

"No, I don't believe so," Olivia said.

Mrs. Olson, a slender, woman with graying hair and lively eyes, shook her head. "We just arrived this afternoon, and we're only staying the weekend."

"That's right." Mr. Olson added. "Tomorrow's our twentieth wedding anniversary." He was a thin fellow and slightly stooped. "We were married in a private ceremony at Mrs. Bow's all those years ago." He turned deep-set eyes to Olivia. "It seemed only natural to mark the occasion by returning to where our journey started and renewing our vows."

"How romantic!" Olivia exclaimed.

"We thought so," Mrs. Olson agreed. "Mrs. Bow's is such an atmospheric place."

"Yes, indeed," Olivia agreed. "And Annabelle makes one feel so welcomed."

"So, if you're free tomorrow at four," Mr. Olson said. "Come join us in the garden room. There'll be a small ceremony with light refreshments afterward."

"Yes, you're all invited," Mrs. Olson added, taking in the elder Crawfords. "That's just the way it was the first time around. All Mrs. Bow's guests turned out, and it was such an intimate and festive affair."

"I'd love to," Olivia said. "Thank you so much." She looked at Lance, and he nodded an affirmative.

"Much obliged for the invitation," Vince said. "We'll surely try to make it."

The crowd had thinned, all the children long since vanished and safely tucked into their beds. The banquet tables had been cleared, the lights dimmed, and Rhett was spinning oldies that felt like good friends. Olivia had melted into her chair, feeling sated and safe.

"I'm going to get a beer." Lance arose from beside her. "Can I get you something, or would you rather blow this joint? We could go to Nesbitt's for a nightcap."

"Not just yet." She smiled at him. "A glass of wine would be nice."

"White?"

Olivia nodded, and Lance looked around at the others seated at the table. "Anyone else?"

"I'm good," Vince said. The rest shook their heads no, and Lance headed off.

Mrs. Olson turned to Olivia. "I understand you're here on business."

"That's correct. I needed to look up some old records both here and in Millbrook."

"Really?" Mr. Olson said. "Why?"

Olivia took a moment to frame her answer. "I am an only child. Growing up, I was told I had no living aunts or uncles, no cousins. My father died when I was very young, and, recently, my mother passed away. It was then that I learned that a relative of mine might be living in this area. Naturally, I was curious, hoping to locate some family member."

"You don't say?" Rudy exclaimed. "What was the name? I know just about every family hereabouts."

"Well, that's the trouble. You see, I'm not sure…"

Suddenly, Rhett was at her shoulder. "Olivia," he said, nodding first to the Crawford brothers and then to Mr. and Mrs. Olson. "Pardon me for barging in."

Vince eyed his brother and gave a slight shrug of his shoulder.

Rhett clamped a fleshy palm on Olivia's shoulder. "May I have this dance?"

Olivia paused to consider. She knew she probably shouldn't, but she was eager to escape the scrutiny and questions, and as always, the music beckoned. "Sure," she said, throwing caution to the wind. She looked about at her tablemates. "Excuse me, won't you?"

Rhett led her to the dance floor, where the opening strains of Michael Bublé's *HAVEN'T MET YOU YET* were sounding, and the two joined the other couples there. For a big man, Rhett was very light on his feet, and Olivia allowed herself to be whisked across the floor. Just as Rhett dipped her, Lance returned to their table, and the glimmer of the liquid in the two glasses he carried caught her eye. The song ended as she returned to the upright position, and Olivia could see Lance looking around, obviously searching for her.

Then he shifted his gaze to the dancefloor, and their eyes met. In that moment, a new track, Maria Carey's smoldering rendition of *I CAN'T LIVE WITHOUT YOU*, blared over the speakers. Rhett tipped his head in a silent question, and feeling somewhat trapped, Olivia responded by once again taking his hand.

At the sight of Rhett and Olivia slow dancing, a vein in Lance's temple throbbed.

He placed the glasses on the table and then strode to the dance-floor. Coming up behind Rhett, he tapped him on the shoulder a bit more aggressively than was called for.

As all of this was transpiring, Vince sat with his arms propped up on the table. At the same time, Rudy pushed away, stretching his long legs before him. The two typically impassive fellows keenly followed the action on the dancefloor, occasionally exchanging amused expressions.

"May I?" Lance's eyes narrowed as he challenged Rhett.

"Being as you brought her, I guess it's your right."

"Damned straight."

Reluctantly, Rhett relinquished Olivia, and Lance took her in his arms. "So long, Olivia, Livia lay ah," Rhett sang. Then he turned away and strutted to the card table to collect his things.

"You need to steer clear of that guy," Lance breathed into Olivia's ear.

"Really? Why? He seems like a nice fellow."

"Yeah. Well, be advised," Lance said, as he twirled her around the dance floor. "Rhett's a real ladies' man. He's broken more hearts than...than I don't know what. You'd best cut him a wide swath."

"How do I know you're not just jealous?" Olivia quipped as she pirouetted back into Lance's arms.

"I *am* jealous," Lance confessed as he cha-cha-cha-ed her across the floor. "But I'm also telling you the truth. You don't want to be another notch on Rhett Dunbar's belt."

Olivia raised her eyebrows and cocked her head, making no promises. "Let's get out of here."

SIX
RENEWAL

Overnight, Crystal Falls had transformed into a winter wonderland. Heavy snow was falling beyond the mullioned bay window in Mrs. Bow's garden room, covering the grounds and frosting the trees and shrubbery. Inside, it was cozy and warm, the room aglow with candlelight. Arrangements of lilies, baby's breath, and white roses graced the windowsills, and a small electric organ had been set up against one wall. Attired in a suit and tie, Clint Olson paced to and fro in a state of agitation.

Annabelle wrung her hands and looked on in consternation.

"It's a catastrophe, utter disaster," Mr. Olson fretted. "I thought we'd planned for every contingency, and now this."

"Surely it's not as bad as all that," Annabelle soothed. "I've sent Lance to call around and see if any of the local organists are available, but at this late hour, and being that tomorrow's Sunday, he's not having much luck."

"What's a wedding without music? My wife's beside herself. She wanted everything to be perfect. It's not as if we'll be doing this again anytime soon." Clint gestured toward the organ. "Don't you play, Annabelle?"

"Not well, I'm afraid. It certainly wouldn't be perfect, although memorable, I can assure you."

Olivia wandered in. Her copper-tinted locks had been swept

up and were held in place with a pearl-studded clip, and she'd donned a black taffeta skirt and a glittery sweater.

"What's the matter?" she asked, catching sight of Mr. Olson's gloomy expression.

"This freak snowstorm has delayed our good friends, Bert and Dede Higden," Clint Olson explained. "They've had to put up in Millbrook, as the highway's been shut down due to the hazardous conditions." He turned toward the window and the swirling snow falling beyond. "Worse yet, the weather system has stalled. There's no telling when this storm will let up."

Lance strode in, shaking his head. "It doesn't look good, folks."

"Oh, dear. That's a shame," Olivia said. "Still, we're here. And Vince and Rudy are on their way."

Annabelle and Clint reacted with grim faces. "And there's more to it than that, I'm sorry to say." Annabelle addressed Oliva. "Mrs. Higden is an organist. She was to play for the ceremony."

"No music," Clint complained. "We might as well be at the office of the justice of the peace."

"Say, I've got an idea." Lance suddenly brightened. "Why don't you do the honors, Livy?"

All eyes turned toward the newcomer.

"Umm," Olivia murmured, her mind racing. "I suppose I could. Just the standard stuff, I imagine. Is that what you were thinking, Mr. Olson?"

The groom-to-be looked mystified. "You know, Wagner's *WEDDING MARCH*, Pachelbel's *CANON in D*, that sort of thing?"

"Why yes." Mr. Olson said. That sounds about right. Could you do that?"

"Sure. Easy peasy," Olivia said, and everyone smiled in relief.

A short time later, the ceremony commenced. Les, Timmy, Vince, Rudy, Annabelle, and a few other townspeople had taken their seats in folding chairs slip-covered in white linen, which had been placed in rows before the bay window. Olivia reigned at the organ, and Chester stood with his back to the window, facing Mr. and Mrs. Olson.

"And so, with the powers vested in me," Chester intoned. "I, once again, pronounce you man and wife. You may now kiss your bride of twenty years."

The guests cheered. Mr. and Mrs. Olson kissed, and Olivia played the *TRUMPET VOLUNTARY* by Clarke.

Afterward, they all reassembled in Charm's parlor, where they were provided with stemmed glasses of Champagne for toasting. Annabelle passed hors d'oeuvres on a silver tray. When she came to stand before Rudy and Vince, she lingered.

"Help yourselves, gentlemen. Looks to me like you could use a little meat on your bones."

"Why, thank you, Annabelle." Rudy plucked a canape off the tray. "They look scrumptious. This is a real treat. Vince and I aren't much in the cooking department."

"Speak for yourself, brother," Vince contradicted. "I can nuke a frozen dinner with the best of them." Annabelle laughed and then feigned a serious demeanor. "Which reminds me. You *are* planning on Thanksgiving, I hope?"

"Aw, I don't know, Annabelle," Rudy said. "We don't want to put you to any trouble—"

"We'd love to come," Vince interrupted. "And thank you kindly for the invitation."

"Goodness knows; it's a standard one," Annabelle clucked. "For heaven's sake. You should just count on it." Once again, she offered Rudy the tray, and this time, their eyes met. It was a brief moment of shared intimacy, but, embarrassed to have witnessed it, Vince looked away. Across the room, Milo, a festive red bandana about his neck, trotted from one guest to another, begging for handouts and, occasionally, scoring.

"Little scamp," Olivia muttered. "Always stealing the show."

Lance followed her gaze and smiled at the dog's antics. "Not true." He turned to her. "You were the star. Did I tell you how amazing you were?"

"More than once." Olivia shrugged off the compliment. "It was a mediocre performance at best. I've played those old standards a thousand times."

"It sounded grand to me, and it certainly meant the world to Mr. and Mrs. Olson. Where did you learn to play like that?"

Olivia chuckled. "My mother was a church organist. As a child, I attended services with her almost daily. I'd sit beside her and watch, fascinated, as her feet danced over the pedals. It was just a natural progression, I guess. I started playing when I was six. I ended up with a BA in music."

"I thought the guitar was your instrument."

"When I was ten, I asked for a guitar for Christmas. Santa didn't disappoint."

"You saved the day, Ms. Barone," Chester said as he and Timmy sidled up.

"That's right," Timmy agreed. "It was a stroke of luck, your being here." Annabelle swooped in just in time to hear the real estate tycoon's words. "Timmy Corker, what utter nonsense," she chided. "Don't you know there's no such thing as coincidence? I believe, with all my heart, that Olivia was right where she was meant to be."

Timmy waved a hand in front of him, as if dismissing this mumbo-jumbo. "Well, I don't know nothing about that, Annabelle. But it does seem things happen for a reason. I'll grant you that."

SEVEN
THANK GOODNESS

I t was Thanksgiving Day, and half the town had assembled in the little white-clapboard, non-denominational church to express their gratitude. The simple altar was adorned with blooms in vibrant fall colors, and the sun shone through the arch-topped, stained-glass windows, casting shards of rainbow hues about the room. Seated between Lance and Annabelle, Olivia fidgeted in the second pew. She'd been in Crystal Falls three weeks now, and she was growing restless; she needed to get on with her life, but she felt stuck somehow. She angled her head to steal a look at Lance. He caught her eye and smiled, and she willed herself to calm down, resolving to take it slow and simply let things play out.

Behind them were Vince and Rudy. Further back and off to one side were Chester and his wife, and Les and Stacey Lowther. Timmy and Lizzy Corker occupied the last pew.

"And so, my dear people," Pastor Peterson said, concluding the thirty-minute service. "We give thanks for the bountiful harvest and for all the many blessings the Lord has bestowed upon us. For even in these difficult times, we are, for the most part, so much better off than so many of our less fortunate brethren. We give thanks for our families and friends, for the community, and for America, where we live out our lives as free men and women, free to choose our destinies in the greatest nation on Earth. Now, let us sing together, *HARVEST HOME.*"

The choir and congregation rose to their feet. Olivia's trained soprano distinguished itself from the other voices, bringing smiles of pleasure to the faces of those around her.

"...bring us all to harvest home. A...men."

The double doors were flung open to a concrete flight of steps leading down to street level. The weather had cleared, the temperatures moderated, and all but a few patches of snow had melted away. The congregants greeted and chattered to one another as they filed out of their pews and surged toward the entrance, each one pausing to thank and shake hands with Reverend Peterson before departing.

When Vince and Rudy came into his line of vision, Peterson's brows shot up. "If it isn't the Crawford brothers. It's been a while."

"Reverend," Rudy nodded.

"To what do we owe this pleasure?"

Rudy's eyes cut to Annabelle.

She graced the pastor with a smile but offered no explanation.

"Uh, no special reason. The crops are in. It's a slow time now. Chores are caught up. So..." Rudy shrugged, uncomfortable at being the center of attention and at a loss for words.

Vince came to his rescue. "Wonderful sermon," he said.

"Mrs. Peterson and I would love for you two, and Lance, of course, to have supper at the parsonage sometime over the holidays."

"Thank you, Reverend," Rudy said. "We'd surely enjoy that."

"I couldn't help but notice, Ma'am," Peterson called to Olivia as she passed before him. "What a beautiful singing voice you have. It seems you're a musical wonder."

"Reverend, meet Olivia Barone, our own Sarah Brightman right here in Crystal Falls!" Timmy Corker exclaimed.

Olivia blushed. "Thank you. I do love to sing."

Lance took Olivia's arm and attempted to steer her away from Timmy, Chester, and Les. But the crowd prevented their escape, and despite his efforts, they were temporarily trapped. Taking advantage of this opportunity, Les nudged Chester, encouraging him to speak out.

"Wait up," Chester cried. "There's something I've been wanting to ask you, Ms. Barone." The five of them slowly inched their way from the nave to the small vestibule. There, they moved to one side, hugging a wall and allowing the other congregants to pass by.

"And what would that be?" Olivia looked from Chester to the dour funeral director.

"Uh, you see…" Suddenly, Les seemed to run out of steam.

Lance stamped his feet and rubbed his hands together in a show of impatience.

"What is it, sheriff?" he asked. "Out with it before we freeze to death."

"It's about the Christmas pageant. Maggie's directed the thing for as long as I can remember. But her health is failing, and she's just not up to it."

"It's like this," Les interjected. "We need somebody talented, somebody with some…some pep, and…personality. You know? To fill Maggie's shoes. The Christmas pageant means a lot to this town."

"That's right," Chester chimed in. "So, naturally—"

Les interrupted. "We were hoping you might step in."

"And help us out in a pinch," the sheriff added. "It would mean the world to us."

Lance's brow bunched. He was an attorney, and his lawyer's brain immediately glommed onto objections to this proposition. But in the next instant, he realized this development might work to his advantage. "I must weigh in. I think that's a great idea," he said, turning to Olivia. "After all, you certainly have all the qualifications. You've got the chops for it, and the kids would surely love you!"

"My goodness." Olivia faced Chester and Les. "I don't know what to say. It's so kind of you to offer, but I'm afraid I'm in no position to take anything on. I'm not sure how long I'll be staying in Crystal Falls." Even as she spoke these words, Olivia was giving their proposal consideration. Just now, she was rudderless.

Directing the pageant might give her purpose, and making music was the joy of her life. She could feel her resolve begin to waver.

"For heaven's sake, Livy, it's just a few more weeks," Lance said. "Why not do it? You said so, yourself, you're a fine musician. I would think directing the pageant would be a piece of cake for someone of your accomplishments."

The sheriff, who loved nothing better than orating, waxed poetic. "Olivia, you realize that sometimes people show up in our lives at just the right moment."

"He's right," Lance added. "Maybe you were supposed to be here for this very reason."

"Come on, Lance," Olivia said. "Aren't you laying it on a bit thick?"

"It's Christmas!" Timmy Corker insinuated himself into the conversation. "What's Christmas without a pageant? You wouldn't want that on your hands, would you?"

"I'm sorry we seem to be badgering you, Olivia," Les said. "But we're desperate. The pageant is a big deal around here. Why the whole town looks forward to it."

"It's the highlight of the holiday season," Chester said. "It wouldn't be Christmas in Crystal Falls without the pageant. People come from all over the county to see it. Tickets sell out every year."

"And the local merchants depend on the revenues it generates," Les added. "No small thing, that. We're under the gun, so to speak."

"I'm flattered," Olivia said, "but…"

"And you'd be paid handsomely," Chester added.

"Very handsomely," Les reiterated. "There's a tidy little annual stipend set aside for the pageant director."

Lance took Olivia's hands in his and gazed into her eyes. "Say yes. I promise you won't regret it. You'd be doing a wonderful thing for the kids…for all of us. What have you got to lose?"

"You'd be helping to keep the spirit of Christmas alive here in Crystal Falls," Chester implored, and Timmy and Les nodded their heads empathetically.

Olivia laughed, capitulating to their concerted cajoling. "Yes! I'll do it. Dear Lord, what have I gotten myself into?"

Chester and Timmy did a happy dance and pumped fists. Lance beamed, delighted that this intriguing woman would be staying on through the holidays.

But Olivia hid a scowl. Writing and producing a two-hour show was a daunting task. Even more terrifying was a question that burned in her brain.

How long could she run and hide from Eric?

EIGHT
SECRETS

Mrs. Bow's dining room table had been set with her finest china, crystal, and silverware, and it was laden with the traditional Thanksgiving side dishes. A pair of antique candlesticks flanked a floral arrangement in fiery fall colors, and the sideboard displayed an array of holiday pies. It was another idealized greeting card image. In the next instant, that image came to life. Laughter and voices raised in animated conversation echoed off the walls as Annabelle, and her guests entered the room. The buxom innkeeper linked arms with Rudy, who seemed both abashed and pleased by her attention. She led him to her table, and the two were followed by Vince Crawford, Timmy and Lizzie Corker, and Les and Stacy Lowther.

Olivia and Lance were the last to enter the room. Rudy drew out the hostess chair, helping Annabelle to be seated, and Lance did the same for Olivia.

"Rudy, you sit at the head of the table," Annabelle said, indicating the chair opposite hers.

"No," Rudy protested mildly.

"Go on." Annabelle gestured.

"You sure?" Rudy asked, but he hastened to do her bidding.

When they were seated, Annabelle spoke. "I want to thank you all for gracing my table. Rudy, would you say the blessing?"

Rudy looked unnerved, and Lance could barely suppress the

laughter that threatened while watching his uncle gird himself for the task at hand. "Ahem," Rudy cleared his throat. "Dear Lord…"

Lance mouthed the words, "Dear Lord," and then rolled his eyes at Olivia. Noting Rudy's distress, she compressed her lips, struggling to keep a straight face.

"We thank you for the harvest's bounty." Rudy looked at Annabelle, and she met his gaze, nodding her approval.

"And for those who have prepared this glorious feast," Rudy continued, seeming to warm to his assigned task. "We thank you for freedom…for our good fortune to live in this great nation, which you have so truly blessed."

Suddenly overcome with emotion, Rudy paused, his eyes taking in all seated at the table. Then he continued. "We ask you to bless those who are no longer with us."

Annabelle and the Crawfords cast their eyes down as emotion played over their faces. Rudy heaved a sigh before continuing. "We thank you for those who have gathered here today, for family and old friends. And we thank you for new friends." He glanced at Olivia. "Bless this food, Lord, to thy purpose. Amen."

"Amen," the others cried.

Timmy, a sparkle in his eye, raised his stemmed glass. "And God bless the cooks!"

All gathered raised their glasses and toasted Annabelle. "God bless the cooks. Here, here!"

"Enough of that," Annabelle said. "Dig in."

Les eyed Olivia over a forkful of turkey. "So, when do you think you'll start rehearsals for the pageant?"

"I've already arranged for the first one to take place on Monday, and I meet with the church keyboardist tomorrow. We've got our work cut out for us."

"Christmas is just around the corner," Lizzy Corker chirruped.

"Yes," Stacy Lowther agreed, her pinched face animated. "Time always seems to fly between Thanksgiving and Christmas."

"It was a stroke of luck for us," Lizzy directed her attention to Olivia. "You coming to town when you did."

"A blessing, indeed," Timmy agreed.

"Don't know what we would have done," Vince said. "Can't imagine canceling the pageant. Christmas wouldn't be the same."

"Luck. Ha!" Annabelle exclaimed. "Luck had nothing to do with it." Annabelle's guests looked at her. "It was fate." She tossed her hands. "How many times must I say it? Things…"

"…happen for a reason," Ruddy and Vince chorused in unison.

"Olivia, have you ever directed a Christmas pageant?" Les asked.

"Oh, yes. I taught music in a high school, and I've directed many concerts and programs over the years." She smiled and arched a brow. "I have an idea for something a bit out of the ordinary, though."

"Do tell," Lizzy cajoled, her blue eyes glinting in anticipation,

"You must," Stacy added, absently putting a hand to her carefully coifed head of dark hair.

"Well, keep it under your hats. I've decided to ask Rhett Dunbar to perform a few numbers from his newest album. I'm quite certain he'll say yes."

Lizzie clapped her small hands in delight, and the others seemed pleased by this announcement. All, that is, except for Lance.

"Rhett Dunbar," he muttered. "Why would you—"

"That's wonderful." Annabelle cut Lance off before he could finish his sentence.

"Rhett's always a big hit. He's almost gotten too famous for our little town."

"I heard he broke up with Courtney Farrow," Vince said.

"That's right," Lizzy Corker piped in. "He's on the market again."

"I thought he was going to marry that one," Stacy added. "They've been an item for what? Three years?"

"The longest of the lot of them, anyway," Annabelle agreed. She leaned in closer to Olivia, filling both their glasses. "There's been quite a succession of young women chasing after our Rhett."

"I guess that makes him the most eligible bachelor in Crystal Falls." Lizzy Corker turned to Lance. "Next to you, that is."

"Not for long," Stacy said. "What do you hear from Meghan, Lance?"

Annabelle, Rudy, and Vince exchanged mortified looks. All the others focused on Lance, who suddenly appeared as though he wished the earth would open up and swallow him whole.

Olivia's smile faded.

"When are you two going to tie the knot?" Stacy asked, blithely oblivious to the discomfort she was causing Lance. "You young people today and your long engagements...for heaven's sake, what are you waiting for?"

The mashed potatoes in Olivia's mouth became a lump of paste impossible to swallow. Her former appetite had been replaced with a queasy stomach, and she pushed her plate away.

Vince clearly read the dismay written on his son's face, and he plunged in, attempting to smooth the troubled waters. Turning to Olivia, he said, "Meghan is...*was* Lance's friend. She's away on a sabbatical in England, researching her second book on 19th-century English poets. We haven't seen her in quite some time. What has it been, son?"

Lance was seething, his jaw set. "Nearly a year," he said through clenched teeth.

Dumbstruck, Olivia sat woodenly.

Annabelle pivoted in her chair and spoke directly to Olivia. "Lance and Meghan were sweethearts all throughout high school. They tried to stay together when they went to college, but with Lance at Harvard and Meghan at the University of Michigan, it just didn't last."

"But then they reconnected at their tenth high school reunion," Vince said. "And picked up where they'd left off."

Lance rose from his chair and leaned in toward Olivia, his fists clenched on the table before him. "But Meghan seemed content to keep our relationship a long-distance one," he said. "Her writing and her research took precedence. I've grown impatient. I want a real, live, flesh-and-blood woman across the dinner table from me, one who thinks that...well, if I'm not more important than those other things, at least I'm worthy of *some* consideration."

Olivia stared at her plate rather than meet Lance's eyes. All the others appeared embarrassed by this intimate revelation and discomfited at the unpleasant turn the heretofore happy occasion had taken.

No one spoke, and the ticking of the grandfather clock in the hallway seemed overly loud and ominous.

Lance broke the silence. "I assumed you all knew," he continued, eyeing his tablemates, one by one. "I've broken it off with Meghan."

Olivia pushed away from the table and rose to her feet. She gazed about at the dinner guests, studiously avoiding Lance's eyes. "Dinner was lovely, Annabelle, and it was a pleasure to see all of you. Please, excuse me, won't you?"

Then she turned and rushed out of the dining room.

Lance made as if to follow her, but Vince grabbed his arm, stopping him in his tracks. "Son."

"Leave her be, Lance," Annabelle said. "She'll come around. She just needs time to think things through."

"I am *so sorry*," Stacy fretted, looking miserable. "I am such a blabbermouth. Forgive me, Lance."

"Me, too," Lizzy added. "Olivia's a lovely girl. I just didn't know…"

Lance sat back down, breathing deeply as he wrested control of his emotions. And then it came to him; if nothing else, Olivia's outburst proved she had feelings for him. "No apologies necessary," he said, a bemused expression crossing his face. "It would have come out sooner or later. Best get it over with."

"You should have been more forthcoming, Lance," Annabelle scolded. "Don't I always say, secrets have a way—"

"…of revealing themselves when we least want them to," Lance grimaced, and the other guests chuckled at his predicament.

"It's been quite a rollercoaster for our Livy," Annabelle explained. "She's got a lot to sort through, just now." The buxom matron eyed Lance. "And there are certain things *she* hasn't been forthright about. I wouldn't beat myself up over this if I were you."

"Is that so?" Lance raised his eyebrows, his curiosity piqued.

"Whatever she decides, I'm sure it'll be for the best. Because, like I always say—"

"Things happen for a reason," Timmy said, finishing her sentence, and they all laughed.

The mood had lightened, all assembled once more appearing at ease. "Let's finish this meal before it gets cold," Annabelle said. "Afterwards, we'll have dessert in the parlor."

The guests gladly resumed eating.

"Annabelle, you are a force of nature," Rudy said.

"I will take that as a compliment, sir."

"As it was meant."

"Happy Thanksgiving, all." Timmy said, raising his glass.

Later that same evening, Lance was back in his familial home at the farmstead, licking his wounds. He paced in front of a roaring fire where the logs crackled and popped as the flames consumed them, casting macabre, glowing fingers over a room awash in shadows.

Vince was seated in his customary chair, a well-worn recliner, situated to the right of the fireplace. Rudy was sprawled in his club chair on the left. Merlin, who lay curled before the fireplace between the two, raised his shaggy head from time to time to huff at whoever happened to be speaking, but for the most part, he remained incommunicado.

"Well, that was a kick in the head," Lance groused. "I guess I got my comeuppance, huh?"

"Aw, son," Vince said. "You were walking straight into a trap."

"What?"

"A man trap," Vince clarified. "Jeez! Did you not see the signs?"

"Uh, no. I saw a pretty lady, someone I'm very fond of, by the way. What are you implying, Dad?"

"Allow me," Rudy interjected. "Your dad's been off the fairer sex ever since your mom passed. God bless her. Such a fine woman, I can't say as I blame him. But that's not fair to you, nephew. So," he turned to his brother and shrugged, silently asking forgiveness for what he was about to divulge.

Vince narrowed his eyes, knowing full well what was coming, but he merely scowled and tossed a hand in the air, giving his sibling tacit permission to continue.

"Lance, neither your dad nor I want you to become as we have—"

"Wait a minute," Lance interjected. "I don't like where this is going. You and Pop made a success of it. I mean," he threw his arms wide, indicating the handsome, lodge-like great room with its massive stone fireplace and open-timbered ceiling. "Look at this place. It's beautiful. And the farm? It has supported our family since, well, for generations.

At that, Merlin shook himself, yawned widely, and then settled back down.

"Yeah. There's the farm. But where are the grandkids? Huh? Where is the life that will sustain this place once my brother and I are rotting beneath this loamy soil?"

"Aw, Rudy," Vince complained. "Give it a rest."

"No. I'm going to speak my peace, brother." Rudy rose from his chair and came to stand before Lance. "I know it's hard for you to understand this, son, but life will not keep throwing you lifelines."

"What?" Lance looked puzzled.

"Find a better metaphor," Vince growled to his brother.

"Let me put it another way," Rudy continued. "There are only so many gold rings the universe presents a man in his lifetime. One day, those opportunities dry up, and you find yourself looking back on a past of what-could-have-been rather than a future full of bright promise. The secret is to know when to grab hold of that golden ring. There are no guarantees. That shiny ring might not bring you what you'd hoped for. It might greatly disappoint, but if you never reach for it, you'll never know. And maybe, just maybe, you'll have missed your golden opportunity."

"So, you're saying?"

"Grab that ring. Go for the gold. Don't follow in my footsteps or those of your father, and let life pass you by."

Lance hunkered before the fire and wrapped his arms around Merlin. "Hey, boy," he said. "What do you think we should do, huh?" He stroked Merlin's silky coat, mulling over his current predicament. Then a thought occurred to him. "So, uncle," he pivoted to face Rudy. "Why did *you* never marry?"

Vince laughed, but there was no humor in it. "Ah, there's a sad tale if ever there was one." He raised his brows and looked pointedly at his brother, whose face had suddenly darkened. "Go on! You tell him, Rudy."

Rudy dragged a palm across his stubbled jaw. "Argh."

"Come on," Lance encouraged. "Out with it."

"He was always in love with Annabelle," Vince blurted.

At those words, Rudy flinched as though he'd been struck.

"There! I've said it," Vince said. "He never had the guts to go after that proverbial gold ring, and now he's a bitter old man, spouting off to you about how you should live your life. Blah, blah, blah!"

Rudy's eyes narrowed. He rose from his chair and crossed to his sibling. "Why, you…"

Vince remained impassive. "You know it's true. Admit it."

"I don't get it," Lance said. "All these years…"

Vince came to his feet and put his face in Rudy's. "All these years he's been carrying a torch for Annabelle, but he was too chickenshit to pursue her. So much for that golden ring. Huh, Rudy?"

Rudy balled up his fist and took a swing at his brother, but there was little determination in it, and Vince grabbed his hand, deflecting the blow. Merlin scrambled to all fours, growling a warning, and Lance leaped to his feet, putting himself between his father and his uncle.

"Alright, alright, you two. Cut it out. Jeez! What the hell is this kind of behavior going to prove? Grow up."

Rudy, a look of scorn on his face, gave his brother a shove and turned away. Vince snorted and crossed to the bar. He withdrew three crystal tumblers from an overhead shelf and proceeded to pour them each a stiff bourbon with bitters. Then he crossed back to Rudy, a glass in each hand. "My peace offering, brother."

Rudy turned to him, conflicting emotions playing over his face. Then he gave a slight nod and accepted the glass.

Lance strode to the bar, palmed the remaining tumbler, and crossed back to his kin. He held his glass before him, saying, "In the words of the bard, *Come, gentlemen, I hope we shall drink down all unkindness.*"

The three clinked glasses, and Vince and Rudy resumed their seats while Lance lowered himself onto a tufted ottoman before the fireplace.

For a time, they sat in silence, each lost in his own thoughts.

Finally, Lance spoke. "Uncle Rudy?" He peered over the rim of his glass at his uncle.

"Yes?"

"Why did you never tell Annabelle of your feelings for her?"

"Aww…" Rudy set his drink on a side table and screwed up his face. "It's complicated." He stared into the fire.

"She was in love with Raymond," Vince explained. "She married him. Hell, Annabelle was the prettiest, smartest, liveliest gal around these parts. All the guys were head-over-heels for her," he said. "Myself included, but then I fell hard for your mom, and that was that. Rudy, on the other hand…" Vince took a long pull of his drink, letting his sentence dangle.

"Okay. I can understand that. But after Raymond died," Lance persisted. "Why didn't you pursue her, uncle?"

"I don't know." Rudy stared into the fire, unseeing. "I didn't think it was proper, I guess. Nor loyal to Ray, for that matter. He was the eldest, and Vince and I looked up to him. It just didn't seem fitting, somehow, lusting after my dead brother's wife." Rudy sniffed and dragged a knuckle over his eyes.

"And then she took up with that scoundrel, Max…what was his name?" Vince glanced at his brother.

"Tibbitts," Rudy said. "A real piece of work. The creep trampled all over her heart and slept with every woman that gave him the time of day. By the time Annabelle got up the courage to leave him—"

"You've got to remember, son," Vince interrupted. "This was

over thirty years ago. Things were different then. Divorce was not nearly so common, and divorced women bore a stigma."

"Yeah," Rudy resumed. "So, she stayed with Max until one day he went too far."

"When she found out he'd been diddling her best friend, that was the final straw, Vince said. "By that time, Annabelle had had her fill of men, and she let that fact be known."

"Let's just say she was not receptive to my advances—"

"Pitiful and uninspired as they were," Vince said, eliciting another scowl from his sibling.

"So, I finally gave it up, ceased, and desisted." Rudy downed the last of his drink and then came to his feet. "Now, if you'll excuse me, I'm off to bed."

Lance sprang out of his chair, crossed to the bar, and grabbed the crystal decanter. "Not just yet. Humor me, uncle," he said, filling Rudy's glass. Vince raised his empty tumbler, and Lance did the same for himself and his dad.

Again, the three sat in silence. This time, it was Vince who broke it. He turned to his brother. "Rudy," he said, his voice impassioned. "Hear me out." Rudy gave an almost imperceptible nod of his head, and Vince continued. "As I said, that was a long time ago. Things change, and people change, too. I believe it is clear to everyone with eyes in their heads that Annabelle is sweet on you."

Rudy appeared momentarily stunned by this statement. "Give me a break," he finally said, obviously buying none of it.

"It's true, Uncle Rudy," Lance said. "Take today, for instance: didn't she insist you sit at the head of the table?"

"That's right," Vince said. "It doesn't take a rocket scientist to figure out what she was implying."

"What?" Rudy asked, his voice hoarse.

"That she wanted you to act as her host, for heaven's sake," Lance said.

"Don't be so dense," Vince said. "It's as plain as the nose on your face; the woman's in love with you."

"No."

"Yes!" Lance and Vince chimed in unison.

"Now, about that golden ring," Vince said. "Isn't it time you got off your keister and reached for the durn thing?"

Lance had retired to his own digs, the little house out back. It was a sweet place. He'd taken pains renovating it so that now, although it maintained its original farmhand house character, the wood plank floors sanded and refinished to a shine, the kitchen and baths updated with Shaker-style cabinetry and antique reproduction fixtures, the entire interior rewired to code, and the gas lights electrified. It was completely modernized and comfortably furnished.

There was only one thing missing.

Seated in his cozy living room before a wood-burning stove, Lance gazed into the glowing embers and pondered his future. Grudgingly, he had to admit that his dad and uncle had given him sound advice. He wasn't getting any younger, and he wanted a family; he didn't want to end up alone like those two. Uncle Rudy had found his nephew's sore spot and scratched it open. Lance knew he'd been biding his time with Meghan, far beyond the point when he'd realized their relationship was going nowhere. But she'd done a number on him, and he hadn't been eager to get back into the dating game and risk the chance of being hurt again. He didn't think his ego could take another beating.

Not until he'd first set eyes on Olivia. That had been a game-changer. And still, he found himself holding back, afraid to put himself on the line again and hazard heartache.

Well, no more!

That woman was the whole enchilada, beautiful, intelligent, talented, kind, and good with kids. He wanted to get to know her better. Learn what her favorite flavor of ice cream was, her favorite color, what sports she enjoyed, where she'd like to go on their honeymoon…

Whoa, buddy! You need to walk a fine line. Don't blow her away by coming on like gangbusters.

The heck with that! He'd damned well better snatch her up before some other bloke did.

Then an image of Rhett working side by side with her flashed into his consciousness. He could picture the big blowhard strumming his ginormous guitar and crooning soppy love songs to a wide-eyed Olivia. Hell, he couldn't sit on his butt and let his chances pass him by like his Uncle Rudy had!

Suddenly, Lance was filled with a sense of urgency.

That's it. I'm going for the gold!

NINE
MAKE WELCOME THE STRANGER

O n this last day of November, the sky was a softly folded, grey blanket of clouds. A brisk wind blew out of the north as winter strong-armed its way into Crystal Falls. The deciduous trees, maple, chestnut, larch, ash, and red and white oak, showed their vexation at this sudden change. They shed their withered, brown, and rust-colored leaves as though eager to be rid of them, and chestnuts and acorns pelted down on the pavement like incoming ordnance.

Olivia glanced at her watch. If she hurried, she'd be right on time for the four o'clock rehearsal. Clumsily, she hiked down the sidewalk, burdened with a handbag over one shoulder, a guitar slung over the other, and a bulky satchel filled with sheet music clutched in both hands. Silently, she berated herself for taking on this assignment. Her situation was tenuous at best. She couldn't stay on at Mrs. Bow's forever.

Am I totally bonkers?

No, you're not, Olivia told herself.

There was no need to overthink this. She'd grown very fond of Annabelle, and the thought of leaving the new friends she'd made here in Crystal Falls made her cringe. The stipend she'd been given to direct the pageant was a generous one, and there was now a tidy sum in her new checking account. Money, at least for the immediate future, was not an issue. Besides, there was nothing she loved more than working with young people and making music. She could almost feel the creative juices flowing in her veins. For the first time in a long time, Olivia dared to feel comfortable in her own skin and hopeful for the future.

She scurried up the sidewalk. As she neared the metal-clad doors of the church hall, she wondered how she'd manage to open them. But before she could begin unburdening herself to free up a hand, she heard footsteps coming up behind her.

"Here, let me," a young girl cried, holding one of the doors open for her.

"Thank you so much," Olivia said. "You're a lifesaver."

"You're welcome," the pigtailed towhead said, making as if to dash on ahead.

"Wait," Olivia cried, and the girl turned back to her. "You wouldn't be going to the Christmas pageant rehearsal, would you?"

"Yes."

"Oh, terrific, I'm Ms. Olivia, and I'm directing. But..." She chuckled self-consciously. "I don't know any of the students participating."

"Well, now you do. I'm Becky Patterson."

"Nice to meet you, Becky."

"Same here. Good luck." Becky scampered away to join her choirmates.

As she stepped from the entry into the practice room, a babble of voices assailed Olivia's ears, and she glanced about owlishly. The church hall was filled with two dozen or more boisterous, chattering children, all squirming in their seats.

"There you are." A gray-haired woman with a weary smile hastened to her side. "It's good to see you again."

"You, too, Mrs. Ellis," Olivia said. "I'd take your hand, but I don't have one to offer."

"Call me Anne." The older woman relieved Olivia of her satchel and set it on a nearby card table while Olivia did the same with her guitar and handbag.

Then she shrugged out of her coat and draped it over a chair.

The organist turned and pointed her chin toward the young-sters. "That's what you've got to work with."

"I'm sure they'll do. Shall we get to it?"

"First, why don't I show you around so that you can get the lay of the land?"

"That would be great!" Olivia exclaimed. "Just let me grab my notebook and a pen."

"As you can see," the older woman said, waving her arms about. "This is a fairly new facility. A lot of thought went into its planning. It's basically a hall with a stage. We have a portable dais which can be used as an altar to accommodate overflow church services." She walked to the left wing. "Up here," she said, climbing the three steps leading to the stage, while motioning for Olivia to follow. "This is where the children will perform."

"Nice," Olivia said, noting the standard red velvet curtain and the rows of foot and overhead stage lights.

"Yes, we rent it out for functions and local productions. So, it's pretty state-of-the-art."

"I'll say." Olivia smiled her approval.

"And come back here." The keyboardist motioned for Olivia to step behind the curtain.

When she did so, the sudden dimness of the cavernous space caused her pupils to dilate.

Glancing up, Anne said, "as you can see, we're all set up for scrims, should you need them." Then she gestured to the right. "The shop's over there, and we've got plenty of risers and lots of other stuff you're welcome to use in the production."

"Wonderful! What about restrooms?"

"Let's take a look." The organist opened a door leading to a hallway off which were both a men's and women's lavatory and dressing room. She pointed down the hall. "And down there is the Green Room where the cast can gather when not on stage."

"This is fabulous. It's a lot more than I expected, Anne," Olivia said, jotting a few notes on her pad. "I am very encouraged."

"I thought you would be," Mrs. Ellis said, a note of proprietary pride in her voice. "Now all we have to do is whip those kids into shape and put together a first-rate production."

Olivia laughed. "That's all!"

The pair made their way back to the stage and then down to the main floor. Then they crossed to an upright piano before which the children were seated.

Once Mrs. Ellis had seated herself on the piano bench, Olivia called out to her. "A few arpeggios, please."

Anne complied, attacking the keys with gusto, and the children settled down and came to attention.

"Hello, everyone," Olivia said when the room had hushed. "I'm Ms. Olivia, and I'm going to be directing this year's Christmas pageant. Mrs. Ellis and I have prepared a program which, we hope, you are all going to enjoy being a part of. Thank you for turning out this afternoon. We have a lot of work ahead of us. So, let's get started. First, why don't we get you arranged from youngest to oldest?" She gestured. "Everyone up."

There was a brief commotion as Mrs. Ellis and Oliva organized the children according to their ages and size: the shortest up front and the tallest in back. Once that had been accomplished, Olivia asked, "May I have two volunteers, please?"

There was a flurry of hands. "Me, me!"

"Okay, Becky Patterson, and…" Olivia pointed to a waif of a dark-skinned girl. She was dressed in worn clothing that looked overlarge and secondhand. The girl hesitated and then darted forward, an eager smile on her elfin face.

"What's your name, dear?"

"Amelie," the girl mumbled, ducking her head shyly.

"Amelie, thank you. You and Becky can hand out the music." Oliva divvied up stacks of sheet music. "Here you go. Make sure everyone gets one copy each." The girls hurried to do Olivia's bidding. "Now then." Olivia clapped her hands, once again calling for silence. "I'm sure you all know the standard carols, SILENT NIGHT, WE THREE KINGS, etc."

"Yes, yes," the children cried in a chorus of eager voices,

"Good. We'll be performing those, of course. But I was hoping to introduce a few new pieces that I think you're going to like."

"Ms. Olivia, Mrs. Olivia!" A freckle-faced redhead, no more than seven-years-old, waved a hand in the air.

"Yes? Your name, please."

"Aiden McGill," the small boy said.

"Well, what is it, Aiden?"

"Can I be a person this year?" The other children erupted in laughter at his question.

"Excuse me?"

"Every year, I'm an animal or a star. This year, I want to be a person."

"The little kids have to be animals and stars," blurted one of the older boys in the back. "It's only fair. Then, when they're bigger, they get to be people."

Other children chimed in, speaking one over the other.

"Yeah!"

"That's the way we've always done it."

"I want to be Mary."

"No, I want to be Mary!"

Olivia raised her palms. "Children," she exclaimed, silencing them. "It's much too early to decide who's going to be what. I need to get to know all of you before any parts are assigned. For now, let's just concentrate on the music. We'll begin with the *BETHLEHEM SONG*."

Oliva picked up her guitar and slipped the strap over her shoulder. "I'll sing it once for you so that you can get the idea." She turned to Mrs. Ellis, indicating that she should play the intro, and the older woman obliged. Olivia strummed her guitar laying in percussive chords, and, at the sound of the syncopated, island style rhythm, the children were instantly captivated.

"Long time ago, in Bethlehem," Olivia sang, "so the Holy Bible say…"

It was mid-morning of the next day, and once again, Olivia found herself in the Crystal Falls Registry Office. As before, there was no one about.

"Excuse me," Olivia called out, ringing the bell on the counter. "Hello!"

Moments later, Celia darted out from the back. "Hello again," she said, offering up a smile. "Did you have any luck?"

Olivia shrugged. "Not really. Although I did find *my* birth certificate."

"Well, that's something."

"Yeah, but my father is still a mystery."

"I thought the name of the birth father was always recorded."

"My father's name is listed as John Smith."

The clerk's face fell. "Oh."

"I'm not looking for any John Smith. I'm quite certain my mom was concealing the true identity of my father. It's so discouraging."

"Gosh, that's a shame," Celia said. "Refresh my memory. What do we know?"

"Let's see…in 1983, when she was nineteen, my mother spent the summer here in Crystal Falls. She stayed with my aunt and uncle, who were childless."

"Why?"

"Not sure. But if I had to guess, I'd say it was some form of punishment, or maybe to take her mind off a boy she was involved with, someone her parents disapproved of."

"I suppose that's possible." Celia nodded. "Anyway, she was here. So, what about your aunt and uncle?"

"Passed away years ago. No other living relatives nearby that I know of."

"Another dead end. No pun intended. What about the man that raised you?"

"He was a great guy, brilliant, an engineer. He died of an aneurysm when I was only thirteen. Boom! One morning, he was there at the breakfast table, and before I'd gotten home from school, he was gone. I loved him very much…" Olivia paused briefly and looked off into space. Then she turned back to Celia. "There was no love lost between him and my mom, though. As far as I could tell, theirs was a cordial but loveless marriage."

"That's terrible."

"I never suspected he wasn't my real father until a few years ago."

"Yeah?" Celia leaned in.

"Mom had started to slip big time; she was in the later stages of dementia, always forgetting things, names, places, me."

"Gee, I feel for you. That must have been awful."

"It was, and it only got worse. But one day, in a rare moment of lucidity, she said to me, *you remind me so much of your father when you do that,* and I asked her what she meant."

"And?"

"Nothing. She was gone again. But it got me to thinking about how things in her past didn't add up. The fact that, as she claimed, I was born premature, that I had no siblings. Something just didn't seem right about it. And then I found the letter."

"The letter?" Celia hung on Olivia's words.

Olivia dug in her bag, eventually withdrawing a yellowed, folded piece of paper. Carefully, she peeled it open, revealing a faded snapshot of a very fresh-faced young couple. The two were seated on the porch steps of a modest, wood-framed bungalow situated on an urban street. Above the pair and to the right of the door, a house number, 635, was prominently displayed. Olivia held the photograph before Celia.

"See, there's my mother."

"Aww…you look like her. Pretty."

Olivia pointed to the young man in the photo. "Don't ask me why, but I'm willing to bet that man is my father."

Celia scrutinized the photo. "Kinda hard to tell what he looks like, huh? That old photograph is overexposed. And with the sun all glary in his face, it could be almost anybody. Besides that, he could be fat, bald, or even dead by now. So, what about the letter?"

"It wasn't until after Mother's funeral when I was sorting through her things that I found this photo. It was stashed away in an old anthology of works by Shakespeare along with a few pressed wildflowers and this letter."

Celia held out her hand. "May I?"

Olivia handed the letter to Celia, and the clerk read it aloud.

"Dear Naomi…" She turned to Olivia.

"My mother's name."

Celia nodded and continued reading.

I just wanted to tell you that I love you, that I'll always love you. That's the truth, and you can believe it. Please, let's just tell your parents and face the music. We can get married. Lots of people younger than us have tied the knot. So, what's to stop us? I know you're afraid that your folks won't allow it, that they won't think I'm good enough for you, which is the truth. And if that's the case, why then we'll simply run away. I'm not afraid of work; I can get a job anywhere. We'll be okay.

P.S. Naomi: I don't want anybody but you. Meet me tonight out by Michael's Field. I'll pick you up, and we can drive somewhere and talk. Yours forever, C."

Celia sighed audibly. "It's so romantic."

"Yeah. Romeo and his Juliet." Olivia shook her head dismissively. "Except, I've got to tell you, my mother wasn't much in the romance department. Quite the opposite, in fact."

"Well, whoever C is...was."

"Not her. She was all about being practical and efficient. And very ambitious to boot. Which, now that I think about it, might be why she didn't pursue Mr. C."

"Humph!" Celia paused to consider. "I suppose that's possible."

"How do I find him?

Celia compressed her lips and paused for a moment in concentration. Then she said, "It's not going to be easy. There must be hundreds of Cs around here."

"That's what I'm realizing." Olivia crossed her arms over her chest. "For instance, there's Chester, the sheriff..."

The two women pondered this possibility. "I don't think so," Celia said. "No family resemblance. Although Chester is a bit of a showman, and I hear that's your thing, too." Her eyes twinkled mischievously as she teased Olivia.

"I'm hardly an extrovert!"

"I suppose. But you *are* a musician. I'm just saying..."

"Uh-huh. I'll take it under consideration."

"What about the Crawford brothers?"

"I hope not!" Olivia's face took on a look of horror. "That could complicate things."

"Why? They're dishy in a rough-around-the-edges sort-of way."

"Believe me," Olivia said. "It wouldn't be good."

"Ooo-kay then. Well, there's Carroll Peterson."

"Who's he?"

"He's the preacher, Reverend Peterson."

The two women looked at one another, eyebrows raised.

"Probably not," Olivia said. "Although Mom *was* the organist at our church."

"Interesting," Celia said. "Ya never know. And then there's Clint Olson. You *do* know who he is?"

"The guy who just renewed his vows? I don't think he actually lived here."

"Oh, right." Then Celia snapped her fingers. "Hey, what about Timmy Corker?"

Olivia gave it a moment's thought before responding. "Seriously, Cee-Cee, the two of us are as different as night and day. But I'm open to it. Tim's a *real* nice guy."

Celia snatched up the photo and peered at it again. She scrunched up her face in concentration. "Hmm...there's always Charlie Nesbitt, the bar owner. He's a handsome fellow, tall and skinny like you."

Olivia leaned in and gazed at the photo, knitting her brows. "It does look a little like him, doesn't it?"

She and Celia exchanged looks of incredulity, and they both broke out in nervous laughter. Suddenly, Olivia was struck by a possibility. "I've got an idea. Is there any way we could check to see whose property is pictured in this photo?"

"Why would you want to do that?"

"I'm pretty sure it's not my aunt's house, because I don't think any of my mother's relatives were aware of her relationship with C. That's pretty much implied in the letter. But it might be my father's house. It seems obvious they were quite comfortable hanging out there."

"I get it," Celia said. "Let me think." She pursed her lips. "Crystal Falls isn't a metropolis. Still, it would be like looking for a needle in a haystack, driving up and down every street searching for this particular house."

Olivia gazed at the photo. "Look," she exclaimed. "There's a house number. Couldn't we narrow down the search by searching for the six hundred block addresses on any given city street?"

"I guess so," Celia said. "But the house in that photo is dilapidated. And that was, what? Thirty years ago? It doesn't look like the place was in the greatest condition back then. By now, it's probably either been torn down or renovated."

"There's got to be something." Olivia looked crestfallen. "I can't believe I've come this far only to be back to square one."

"I've got a proposition," the clerk said, a conspiratorial grin on her face. "It's a real slow time around here, the weeks before Christmas through New Year's." Celia placed a palm on Olivia's wrist. "Let me help you."

"Gladly."

"Maybe we could research old newspapers to see if that property is pictured in any photographs."

"That's a great idea. When can we get started?"

Cee-Cee glanced up at the wall clock. "It's getting late. Let's go at it tomorrow. Don't get your hopes up, though, It's still a long shot. But then again..."

"Ya never know," Olivia cried, gathering up the photograph and letter. Once they were stowed in her satchel, she leaned into Celia, dropped her voice, and spoke to her in a stage whisper. "Please, don't breathe a word of this to anyone."

Celia pressed her right thumb to her pointer finger and drew them across her mouth. "My lips are sealed!"

TEN

WILL WONDERS NEVER CEASE

Two hours later found Olivia in a much-altered state of mind. She was dashing about her room, collecting personal items, and tossing them into an open suitcase set atop the bed. Milo lay curled next to it, following her every move with troubled eyes.

"This is madness," Annabelle complained. The curvy matron was seated at the vanity table, watching Olivia's meltdown with a look of consternation on her face. "You can't leave now. The children are counting on you to direct the Christmas pageant. The entire town is depending on you."

Olivia turned to Annabelle. "That's all well and good. But Eric's been calling non-stop."

"Which is perfectly understandable."

"Yeah. But in his last message, he said he'd located me and was coming after me."

"He's bluffing."

"Maybe." Olivia reached for her cell and brandished it. "But do you know what this is?"

Annabelle nodded.

"No, you don't. It's the next best thing to a GPS." Olivia flung herself on the bed, and Milo grumbled in protest. "I've been careful. I haven't used my credit cards." She shook her phone. "But I've used my cell."

"You're safe here."

"I'm not! I haven't been safe anywhere...for so long... You don't understand. My husband is a powerful man. He has friends in high places, people who can make things happen, and no one the wiser. I have to get out of here."

Annabelle rose and crossed to Olivia. She plunked down next to the frightened woman and took her quaking hands in hers.

"Look at me," she commanded.

Olivia cut her eyes to Annabelle's.

"Give me your phone."

"Why?"

"Because it's going somewhere far away from here, that's why."

"But all my contacts, my stored numbers..."

Annabelle narrowed her eyes. "Livy, even I know how important that information is to you. Save it all to the Cloud. And anything really crucial, account numbers, passwords, write them down. I'll drive you to Millbrook tomorrow, and you can buy a new phone."

Olivia shuddered.

"Have you told Lance?"

"I couldn't." Olivia held her head in her hands. "I'm so ashamed. I told him my husband had passed away. You didn't say anything to him, did you?"

"Of course not. But I don't think he'd be shocked at your circumstances. Lance might come across as easygoing, but he's no fool, Livy. It's none of my business, but I think that man deserves to know what you've been dealing with. We've all taken a shine to you, dear. And secrets have a way of revealing themselves when we least want them to."

Olivia processed this information and nodded. But then she was struck by a new possibility and once again plunged into despair. "When Eric finds out he's been duped, he'll come here. Then what?"

"Don't you worry about that," Annabelle reassured. "When and if the time comes, we'll have our own little plan of defense in place. We're not going to let you be run out of here. If we do, it'll never stop. You'll be running from that man forever. We must put the kibosh on it. Don't think that your soon-to-be-ex-husband is the only one with friends in high places."

Annabelle gained her feet and affected a no-nonsense demeanor. "Now, back up that pesky, black tracking device to the Cloud." She gestured to the bed. "Put those things away, and then come down and have some dinner with me. We'll have turkey soup, leftover dressing, and wine. Afterward, you can help me decorate the Christmas cookies, and we'll have more wine. If we're lucky, we'll hit the sack before midnight."

Light snow was falling, dusting the denuded trees with a gleaming white rime and clinging heavily to the boughs of the evergreens. With its brick-fronted shops and cobblestone streets, Crystal Falls' main thoroughfare looked like a Burl and Ives Christmas card.

Nesbitt's severed hand sign shone brightly, but at this late hour, the street was deserted, the tavern shuttered and empty. Inside, in the upstairs apartment fronting the back alley, Charlie Nesbitt lounged in his leather recliner perusing a newspaper, an overfed tabby purring at his feet. The apartment was spartan, for there were no signs of a woman's touch here, but it was cozy and clean. A large flat-screen TV was tuned to a college football game. From time to time, Charlie lowered the newspaper to glance at the screen and grumble half-hearted comments at the fumbled plays.

"Aw, for cripe's sake, you jackass, run with the ball. No, no, no! Argh." Charlie tossed the paper aside and addressed the cat. "What do you think, Alley? Watching paint dry is more exciting than this, huh?"

Charlie scooped the cat up, and the black and white striped feline settled into his lap, purring loudly when he stroked her back.

"Thata girl. We're a fine pair, aren't we? Two old geezers just lying around with nothing particular to do and nowhere to go. And that's just the way we like it, isn't that right, Alley? Just the way we like it."

Charlie rose from the chair and gently set the cat on the rug. "Come on," he said. "Let's go scrounge us up some supper. We'll have us a feast. I brought up some Kosher corned beef and a few slices of aged Swiss cheese. Gonna fry us some Reuben sandwiches. That sound good, Alley?"

The cat yawned and then licked a paw.

"You betcha it does." Charlie crossed to his compact kitchenette. On the way, he glanced at a framed photograph on a side table and stopped up short. The image was of an attractive young woman seated on a porch stoop.

"And goodnight to you, my beauty," Charlie said. "Be well, my love."

Far to the north of Crystal Falls, a long-distance freight hauler wheeled his semi down a nearly deserted highway. He was road weary and muttering. "I'm either intrepid or crazy to be out here on a night like this."

The wind was howling, and snow whirled about, reducing his visibility to little more than zero. David Lampkin leaned forward in his seat, hands gripping the steering wheel. He squinted, cussing silently under his breath as he peered out over the windshield. But it was no use; he couldn't see a damned thing.

"Gosh darn it, I'm getting too old for this," he groused.

He turned on the wipers, and that helped some. In the beam of his headlights, the pelting snow glistened like diamonds, nearly blinding him with their dazzle. Yet, for all the beauty of this winter's night, a feeling of desolation washed over him. When he made out the REST AREA sign on the shoulder, he breathed a ragged sigh of relief. Flicking on his blinker, he pulled off the highway into a sprawling, well-lit, super truck-stop plaza. No visitor center had ever looked so inviting.

Or as safe.

After parking the big rig, David leaped down from the cab. Hunching his shoulders against the stiffening gale, he barreled toward the plaza. There, housed under one large, welcoming roof, were restrooms, a fully stocked mini-mart, and a restaurant. He made a beeline to the market. Inside, tucked into a corner, was a miniature US Post Office, just as he knew there would be. He strode to the counter and dug a small mobile device out of his pocket. Holding the black object in his palm, he turned the ROAM setting on and stepped up to the counter.

An attractive brunette in her late thirties smiled wearily over the counter at him. "Hello there. Some weather, huh?"

"Brutal," he agreed. "I'd like to mail a package."

"Certainly. That's what I'm here for."

"Figured as much." He handed her the phone Miss Annabelle had given him.

"No problem. I'll wrap it in some paper and put it in one of these little flat rate packages, okay?" She selected a small envelope and held it up for him to inspect. "See, it's got a little bubble wrap padding."

He nodded. "That'll do."

"Oh, I have a plastic sandwich bag from my lunch. Lucky you." She wrapped the phone in paper, placed it in the plastic baggie, and fitted it into the box. While she performed these tasks, the trucker withdrew a slip of paper from his pocket.

"Here's the address where it's to be mailed."

The woman read the address aloud while keying it into her computer. "Regular post would cost you eight dollars and twenty-five cents. But this is a flat rate at fifteen dollars, and it'll be there in three days, guaranteed." She looked up at him, a rueful grin on her face. "Unless, of course, this weather keeps up."

"Priority's fine." He placed a twenty-dollar bill on the counter.

"Rough, having to work over the holiday," the woman said as she quickly collected his money and made change.

"It's okay. I've got no family. So, what's the difference? Besides," he gave her a resigned smile. "Here you are doing the same."

"The good news is I'm off in a few minutes." She handed him a receipt. "If you're hungry, the food's first-rate at the café. Nothing fancy but good home-cooking."

"I could eat a horse."

"Not on the menu, but I highly recommend the brisket."

"Being as you think so highly of it, why don't you join me? My treat." He gave her his best hang-dog-look, and the woman considered his offer. "C'mon, what do you have to lose?" he coaxed, turning on the charm. "I sure would like the company."

She grinned, and in that moment, he thought she looked like a schoolgirl.

"Oh, why not? It's the best offer I've had all day."

An hour and a half later, it had nearly stopped snowing, and the stiff wind had abated. For all the storm's bluster, there was little accumulation on the ground to remember it by. The truck driver and postwoman exited the plaza, their heads together as they chatted companionably. Abruptly, they stopped in their tracks, suddenly cognizant of the two police cars, their lights flashing, conspicuously parked, front and center, in the parking lot.

Other travelers eyed the police cars curiously as they passed by on their way to and from the plaza. A pair of uniformed state troopers walked between the vehicles parked in the lot, shining bright beams from their flashlights into the interiors. Two others, stationed at either side of the plaza, scrutinized the visitors as they came and went.

David smiled grimly and gave a slight nod of his head. His face registered no surprise.

"I wonder what's up with that?" the postwoman said.

He shrugged and then turned to her. "Well, Lisa, it's been real nice getting to know you."

"You too, David. Thank you for dinner."

"I should be back this way in a week or so."

"Here, give me your cell phone," Lisa said, and David reached into his pocket and handed it to her.

Deftly, she recorded her phone number in his address book.

"Do this thing regularly, do you?' he asked, grinning wickedly.

Lisa frowned, offended. "Only for my kids' friends," she snapped. "What do you think I am?"

David held his palms before him. "Okay, okay. Sorry. Jeez! It was a joke, that's all. You gotta believe me, I didn't mean anything by it."

"Humph! Anyway—"

"So, I'll call you."

"You do that," Lisa said, somewhat mollified.

"And maybe then I could take you on a *real* date."

"Maybe." Now, she was playing hard to get, and David smiled at her indulgently. Then he bent down for a quick, chaste kiss.

But Lisa wrapped her arms around his neck and drew him to her, demanding more. Just as quickly, she released him. "So long, David." She turned and sauntered toward the parking area, her high-heeled boots making a satisfying clicking sound on the concrete pavement.

David watched as she sashayed past a policeman. Before turning away, the trooper paused and eyed the woman's shapely figure.

Lisa unlocked the driver's side door to a late model, sporty-looking Honda Civic and climbed in. As she closed the door, she pivoted to face him and raised a hand in farewell. "Bye-bye, Dave."

David returned the gesture. "You drive safe, now."

Lisa closed the car door, started the engine, and backed out of the parking slot with practiced efficiency.

David remained rooted to the spot, never taking his eyes off the woman who was probably going to save his life. He followed her progress until she turned onto the on ramp and disappeared. Smiling at his good fortune, he strode to his rig, murmuring, "Will wonders never cease?"

Fifty-one hours after Olivia had handed off her cell phone to Annabelle, found the two of them seated at opposite ends of the innkeeper's kitchen table, dozens of decorated sugar cookies on sheets of waxed paper spread before them. Annabelle dipped an index finger in a nearly empty bowl of icing and popped the digit into her mouth. "Well, that's the lot of them," she said. "Between the three batches we made the other night, I'd say we're well-stocked. Time for wine."

"Ugh, I don't care if I never see another sugar cookie," Olivia said. "Wine sounds good, though."

"Ha!" Annabelle gained her legs, crossed to the kitchen counter, and proceeded to uncork a bottle of white. "Pinot okay with you?"

"Perfect." Olivia gathered up the bowls of frosting and carried them to the sink.

"Just put them in the dishwasher," Annabelle instructed. "I'll store the cookies in containers once the icing's set."

"Yes, ma'am." Olivia did as she was told and then sat back down at the table. "Do you know, yours were the first Christmas cookies I ever decorated?"

"No!" Annabelle placed a wineglass before her and proceeded to fill it.

"Uh-huh. Mom wasn't much for holiday baking, but we always had a beautiful tree."

"Every family's different." Annabelle poured herself a glass of wine and then set the bottle at the end of the table.

"Here's to you." Olivia raised her glass in a toast. "You saved me."

"Hardly." Annabelle pulled a chair across from Olivia's. "But right back at you, dear." Annabelle clinked glasses with Olivia. "It's been wonderful having you here." She patted Olivia's hand. "You're like the daughter I never had."

"And you're like the mother I always wished for."

"A compliment, indeed." In the next instant, Annabelle seemed to grow pensive. "So, as someone who cares for you, and doesn't mean to meddle...would you mind if I speak frankly?"

"Of course not."

Annabelle set her glass down and paused, gathering her thoughts. Then she looked hard at Olivia, "Please don't take offense."

"Definitely will not." Olivia's brows knit up, nonetheless.

"I realize you've been through a lot, that your faith in men has been shaken."

Olivia nodded. "True."

"Given my own unfortunate history, my man troubles, so to speak, I believe I'm uniquely suited to offer advice."

"Go for it. God knows I'm in a quandary."

"Okay, here it is: Don't let a bad experience sour you on the male species."

"Uh-oh!" Olivia took a sip of her wine. "You're on to me."

"I'm dead serious." Annabelle looked away, momentarily lost in another time. Then she turned back to Olivia. "If you do, you might fail to recognize the very best thing to have ever come your way."

"Lance?"

"Precisely. Livy, I understand how you might feel that now's not the right time to be embarking on another relationship." Olivia nodded, and Annabelle continued. "But I want you to think about something. Will you humor me?"

"Annabelle, I would do anything for you. What is it?"

"How was it that you landed in the Crawford hayfield?"

"A momentary lapse in concentration," Olivia said. "If you must know, I'd flipped down the visor to take a quick peek at my shiner. That was all it took."

"The black eye. Umm…" Annabelle came to her feet, snatched up her wineglass, and rounded the table. Taking the seat next to Olivia, she said, "Okay. And the fact that Lance just happened to be out for a ride and witnessed your accident?"

"It was a pretty great coincidence. I'll grant you that." Olivia brought her glass to her lips and drank deeply.

"And another great coincidence that he brought you here to me. Right?"

"I'll say. Lucky me!"

"And that you just so happened to land here in Crystal Falls when the town needed a musician capable of directing the Christmas pageant?"

"I see where you're going with this…" Olivia jumped to her

feet, grabbed the wine bottle, and carried it to their end of the table. "May I?" She held it suspended over Annabelle's glass.

"Yes, please."

Olivia poured them both another glass and then resumed her seat. They clinked glasses. "To happy coincidences!"

"More than coincidences," Annabelle said. "The fact that you were here on the very weekend of a freak storm and were able to step in and provide music for the Olson's renewal of vows?"

"Yup, another one. Quite a pattern, huh?"

"And let's not forget that Lance is besotted with you."

Olivia laughed dismissively. "A harmless flirtation."

"It's much more than that, and you know it. I realize people often don't take me seriously, that they think I'm a foolish old woman who believes in signs and hocus-pocus."

"That's not true," Olivia protested.

"I don't care what people think." Annabelle took Olivia's hand in hers. "Livy, are you a woman of faith?"

"I'm not a regular churchgoer, if that's what you're asking."

"It's not. Do you believe in God, a higher power?"

"Absolutely," Olivia said.

"In that case, I'll let you in on a little secret; I have angels all around me."

Olivia sobered, looking taken aback. "Really?"

"I think we all do, but I'm particularly attuned. I believe things happen for a reason, that there are no coincidences in life. And Livy?"

"Yes?"

"I believe with all my heart that you are at exactly the right place at exactly the right time. You have been accepted into our close-knit community with open arms and thoroughly embraced. That's unusual."

"It's true. I feel blessed."

"Because you have been, dear." Annabelle squeezed Olivia's hand and released it. "My last piece of advice to you…"

"What is it?"

"Stop thinking with your head and start trusting your heart. Of course, I'm partial…but Lance is a wonderful man, brilliant, hard-working, principled, solid. And all of those qualities are wrapped up in a very attractive package, you must admit."

"He's dreamy, alright."

"More than that, he comes from good stock. The Crawfords are fine, upstanding people. I'm telling you, Livy, men the caliber of the Crawfords are few and far between. Don't make the same mistake I did and let this opportunity slip between your fingers because you think the timing isn't right. I'm certain, if you take into consideration all of your *coincidences*, you may be surprised to find that the timing for *this* romance is well neigh perfect."

Olivia sat quietly with her head bowed as Annabelle's words resonated in her cranium. Then emotion flooded over her, and her face crumpled. In the next instant, she was weeping uncontrollably.

"Oh, darling," Annabelle consoled. "I'm sorry to have upset you." She bounded out of her chair, snagged some paper towels from off the roll, and offered them to Olivia. "There, there," she soothed as the tears coursed down Olivia's cheeks. "Let it all out. You've been bottling up all those feelings for far too long."

Once the floodgates opened, the waterworks flowed, and Olivia seemed incapable of turning them off. At a loss, Annabelle picked up a cookie and held it before the distraught woman. "Here. Have a cookie."

At those words, Olivia's emotions seesawed. Suddenly, she was alternately laughing and hiccupping. "A cookie?" she croaked between peals of laughter. "But I said I never wanted to see another cookie."

"Try it," Annabelle insisted. "A cookie makes everything better."

Olivia snatched the cookie from Annabelle and took a huge bite. "Umm...delicious," she mumbled as she chewed, pausing only to wipe her runny nose. "You're right," she said, after swallowing hard. "How come nobody ever told me that?"

ELEVEN
MAY THE BEST MAN WIN

I t was a brilliantly bright, sunny day, the sky a deep cerulean blue. Light poured through the windows of the church hall, the mounds of glistening snow outside seeming to intensify the radiance. Rhett and Olivia were perched on stools in front of the stage, guitars in hand. Olivia strummed a chord and sang:

"Christmas comes but once a year, Santa Claus and his reindeer." The sound of the last cord hung in the air. Olivia looked at Rhett. "Like that?"

"Close. I'm thinking something more like this." Rhett repeated the lyric, but this time with a syncopated beat. "And then the kids could come in with the chorus."

Olivia played and sang the phrase, this time mimicking Rhett's rhythm. Then she turned to him, her eyes gleaming. "You are a genius! I can't thank you enough for doing this, Rhett."

"My pleasure, pretty lady." Rhett glanced at his watch. "Hey, it's not quite five-thirty. The kids don't get here till seven. How about we grab a quick bite at Nesbitt's?"

"Sounds good." Olivia jumped to her feet. "But we're going to have to hustle."

Rhett lifted the guitar strap off his neck and placed the instrument next to its case on a folding chair, and Olivia followed suit.

"Hustle your bustle, babe. I'm starving," he said.

"It'll be good to take a quick break. Recharge." Olivia shrugged into her coat.

Immensely pleased with himself, Rhett ogled Olivia from behind. For a brief moment, he considered making her his meal.

The two walked abreast down Main Street, so close their bodies brushed against one another from time to time. But they were not ambling. They quick-stepped in unison, angled against the cold and steering toward Nesbitt's, where the severed hand sign glowed like a welcoming beacon. When, at last, they'd gained the entrance, the whoosh of heat and the mouth-watering aromas that enveloped them nearly bowled them over.

Nesbitt's, it appeared, was a popular destination for a cold day. Even at this early hour, the place was nearly full to capacity. No sooner had they crossed the threshold than Chester Parker, Les Lowther, and Timmy Corker raised their beer mugs and shouted greetings from the bar.

"Ms. Olivia!" Charlie rounded the bar. "Rhett! I have a booth by the window with your names on it."

"How are you, Charlie?" Rhett slid into the booth.

"Not bad. I can't complain. And you?" Charlie placed two menus on the table.

"Doing great. This siren bewitched me." Rhett gazed at Olivia. "And, before I knew what was happening, she'd enlisted me to help with the Christmas pageant."

Olivia scooted into the seat opposite Rhett, shaking her head.

"Not true! This is how rumors get started." She shot Rhett a warning look.

"Is that so?" Charlie's eyes rested on Olivia. "Some kind of magic, that," he murmured. "I'll be back in a few minutes to take your orders."

Despite her best intentions to enjoy the present company and put thoughts of Eric and Lance from her mind, Olivia couldn't ignore the warning bells clanging in her belfry.

"What is it?" Rhett asked, noting her sudden consternation.

"Nothing," Olivia reassured him. "I'm just going to powder my very shiny nose." She slipped out of the booth and dashed for the lady's room. But try as she might, she couldn't banish the melody that played in her head, *Olivy, Livy lay ah!* But this time, the ditty ended on a discordant note.

Say nah!

Several blocks away, Annabelle bustled about in her well-stocked kitchen, preparing one of her favorite winter stews. Milo dozed on a rag rug she'd placed before the hearth, but a loud rapping on the side door roused him, and he barked a high-pitched warning.

"Quiet, Mr. Milo!" Annabelle shook a finger at him and crossed to the door. "Hello," she trilled, opening the door. But her smile faded at the sight of a very forlorn-looking Lance standing on her stoop, two empty casserole dishes in hand.

Annabelle waved him in. "Come inside. You're blue."

"In more ways than one."

"What brings you out on a day like this?"

Lance bent to brush his lips against her cheek. "I'm just returning your casseroles, is all."

Annabelle closed the door behind Lance and relieved him of the dishes. "Thank you, Lance," she said, setting them on the counter. "Did you enjoy the leftovers?" She turned and motioned for him to sit at the kitchen table.

"Delicious! I believe I've gained five pounds. And what's that you're cooking?" he asked, unbuttoning his coat, and taking a seat. "It smells heavenly."

"Hungarian goulash." Annabelle turned back to tend the pot on the stove.

"You are an amazing cook, my favorite Auntie-in-all-the-world."

"Humph! Your only Auntie. How are your dad and uncle?"

"They're fine. How's Olivia?"

Annabelle stopped stirring the pot and faced him. "She's hanging in there. Been spending a lot of time with Rhett Parmer."

The matron tossed her head, making light of this revelation. "There's nothing to it. You know they're working on the Christmas pageant."

Lance reeled as though from a blow. "Aw, hell!" He rested his elbows on the table and buried his head in his hands. "I knew it. I knew that louse would be a problem. Damn it!"

Annabelle crossed to Lance and rested a hand on his shoulder. "It's okay, darling. It truly is. I know it doesn't seem so now. But trust me. This is all going to work out splendidly." But then her voice took on a discordant note, and she glared at him. "So long as you shake off your ennui and attend to business."

Lance shook his head as if to clear it. "Oh, yeah? This is just ducky. She's with that charmer…that rogue. What am I to do?"

"You've always envied Rhett. It's very unattractive."

Lance ejected from his chair. "The man is toying with the girl I love!"

Annabelle said nothing, letting Lance's words sink into his consciousness. Not until she thought they'd resonated did she break her silence. "Well, there you go. And what do you propose to do about *that*?"

"Gosh darn it, Auntie A, I don't know. You're the one with all the answers. What do *you* suggest?"

"I swear. You men are clueless when it comes to matters of the heart," she exclaimed. "Tell her how you feel about her, for heaven's sake. Trying to make Rhett look bad in her eyes will only backfire. He's a very charming and talented fellow. Unfortunately, he just can't seem to stay in a relationship. But that's of no consequence. It's not about him."

Annabelle drew away and looked Lance in the eyes. "I'm not one to reveal confidences, but I will say this, Olivia hasn't been completely honest with you either, my dear. In her defense, she's been badly hurt, and she has serious trust issues. You need to clean the slate and start fresh. And don't push her. She's been pushed around enough." Annabelle patted his cheek before returning to the stove. "And that's all I'm going to say about the matter. She'll have to tell you the rest."

"That's all well and good, but first, I have to get her to agree to *see* me. It's been a week and not a word from her."

Annabelle continued stirring the pot on the stove. "It'll all work itself out, Lance. You'll see." She turned to him. "Here, come and taste this for me." She held out a spoonful of stew. "What do you think? Does it need salt?"

Dutifully, Lance crossed to Annabelle and tasted the savory concoction. "Umm!" Despite his ill humor, he smacked his lips. "Perfecto. Put a generous helping of *that* in one of those casserole dishes for me, won't you? God knows I can't stomach another TV dinner."

Olivia sat before a spartan worktable intent on a computer monitor in the Records Depository of the Crystal Falls County Courthouse. Her head was angled, her face close to the flickering screen as she viewed a spool of images scanned from the local newspaper. She clicked from one image to the next, her brow furrowed in concentration.

Celia emerged from the back and crossed to Olivia. "Having any luck?"

Olivia turned a troubled face to Celia. "No, but I'm fast becoming an expert on the history of Crystal Falls."

"Ha!" Celia exclaimed. "Lotta good that'll do you."

"Actually, it's pretty interesting. I haven't found the house, but I've dug up heaps of information about several possible Cs."

"No kidding? Like what, for instance?"

"Like the fact that Chester Parker's been reelected sheriff for three consecutive terms. I guess he's pretty popular."

"That he is. Besides, he's honest and fair. And that's saying a lot for a small-town politician. For any politician, for that matter. One could do worse. What else?"

"That the Crawford brothers are fourth generation."

"It's true. One of the oldest and most respected families around here."

"Humph!" Olivia snorted. "And that Timmy Corker's story is a rags-to-riches tale. How he turned one small mom-and-pop grocery into a high-end shopping center, and the rest is history."

"Oh, don't let Timmy's cherubic mien fool you. He's shrewd, alright. That man owns more prime real estate holdings in the three-county area than anyone I know. Though he doesn't flaunt it, he's a millionaire many times over."

Olivia raised her brows, digesting this information. "Carroll Peterson left for the seminary about seven months before I was born."

Celia's dark eyes grew round. "Yipes!"

"Haven't come across much on Charlie Nesbitt, other than the fact that he enlisted in the Marines about the same time Carroll Peterson went off to Divinity School."

"Well, that's troubling," Celia admitted. "Charlie keeps to himself. He does most of his socializing at Nesbitt's, mixing work with pleasure, although he does come out and support the local causes. The man's a bit crusty but sweet. I wouldn't let that hard exterior fool you; he's an old softie at heart."

Olivia nodded. Then she turned back to the computer monitor. "Oh, and I've discovered a whole slew of other Cs that need investigating."

"Wonderful!"

"Not really."

Celia pivoted and crossed to the counter.

Olivia continued her perusal of images on the screen. Then suddenly, she stopped, and reverse clicked. "*Wait!* Wait, wait, wait. What is this?"

Celia turned on her heel and doubled back to Olivia. Bending down, she peered over her new friend's shoulder to better view the computer monitor. "What am I looking at?"

"See that?" Olivia pointed to an image on the screen. Depicted there was the same house as in her photo, the house number 635 clearly visible. It sat before a street flooded with water that rose halfway up the steps leading to the front porch. Two young boys were having the time of their lives, playing in a small inflatable raft that had been tethered to the porch railing.

"Oh, my goodness," Celia exclaimed. "That's it!" She leaned in closer and read the caption aloud. "A week of unseasonably heavy rains has turned many thoroughfares in Crystal Falls and outlying areas into waterways navigable only by boat. Pictured is the home of Nathan and Walda Corker. Their son, Timmy, and his playmate are making the most of this unusual event."

Celia and Olivia turned to one another, their mouths agape. Then they spoke at the same time. "Timmy Corker!"

TWELVE
RUMBLE

Olivia was in high spirits as she swept through the door of the courthouse and out into the blustery day with a new spring to her stride. "I can't believe it. Timmy Corker," she muttered. "A loveable guy, no kids to hate me, and an extremely successful businessman...a girl could do worse!"

After stuffing her notepad into her bag, she skipped down the icy steps, not paying particular attention to where she was going. At the same time, Lance, briefcase in hand, a cell phone to his chin, was charging up those steps. He happened to glance up just as Olivia looked down, and before Olivia could gather her senses and attempt to change course, the two came face to face.

"Olivia!" Lance cried.

Olivia turned away, vainly searching for a means of escape.

But Lance side-stepped her. "Olivia, please. Just one minute of your time. I beg you."

Olivia couldn't ignore the pain in his eyes, and her resolve crumbled. Lance took her arm, and she allowed herself to be led down the steps. He steered her to a bench affixed to the pavement at street level, and the two sat. Olivia averted her eyes, hesitant to wade into this quagmire, but Lance had no such qualms.

"First, let me say how truly sorry I am. I should have been upfront with you about Meghan from the very beginning. But... well, I didn't know how...how much you were going to mean to me. Surely you realize it was just a lark at first, a fun, easy flirtation...no strings attached, and—"

Olivia shook her head and interrupted. "You don't have to do this, Lance. It isn't necessary."

"But it is. Because..." He took her hands in his. "You see, I'm falling in love with you."

"Oh, Lance—"

"No. I have to say it. I am going to be perfectly truthful with you from now on."

Olivia gazed into his open face and was immediately wracked by guilt. "Lance, I..." Her voice hitched with suppressed emotion. "I haven't been entirely upfront with you about my situation, either."

Gently, Lance touched her face. Gazing into her eyes, he said, "I've got all the time in the world. Nothing could be more important."

"But don't you have to be in court or something?"

"No. I'm just filing a brief. I can have my paralegal do it tomorrow. Let's go somewhere warm, someplace where we can talk." His hand fell from her face and came to rest upon hers. "Please."

Olivia bit her lip as she pondered his proposal. Lance was so solemn, his eyes pleading. Suddenly, she wanted to unburden herself of her secret. "Alright," she agreed. "Let's do this."

Fifteen minutes later found them at Nesbitt's. Olivia and Lance sat across from one another at one of the prime booths by the window. They were unbuttoning their coats and settling in when Charlie swooped in with menus.

"Hiya, Lance." Charlie raised his eyebrows, shooting a question at Olivia, but she merely shrugged. Charlie winked at her conspiratorially. "You're getting to be a regular around here."

Olivia blushed, recalling her recent meal with Rhett. But Charlie didn't pursue that topic, and Olivia laughed nervously in relief. "And why not?" she asked. "You can't beat the food. And the service? Why it's almost *too* attentive."

Charlie snorted. "And what man worth his salt wouldn't pay attention to a pretty gal, huh? I ask you, Lance?"

Lance smiled tightly but offered no comment.

Charlie held the menus before them. "You two know what you want?"

Lance looked at Olivia.

"Just coffee for me," she said.

"Make that two," Lance added.

"Oh, I'm going to the bank on this one," Charlie chortled. "Going to buy me a chateau on the French Riviera." He crossed to the bar, and rather than look at one another, Lance and Olivia followed his retreating figure. An awkward silence fell between them until, finally, their eyes met. Then they both spoke at once.

"I'm sorry we got off to…" Lance said.

"It's like this. I never meant…" Olivia blurted. "Sorry."

"No. Ladies first."

"My husband isn't dead."

"I never believed that he was."

"What?" Olivia sat up straight.

"I'll shut up. You go."

Beneath the tabletop, Olivia wrung her hands. "Where to start?"

"When did the trouble begin?"

Olivia gazed out the window, her eyes unfocused. Then she turned back and continued. "After university, I landed a teaching position in an exclusive private school, St. Andrews Academy. Located in an upscale community, the campus was a forty-five-minute commute from the city. Assuming the title Assistant Director of Music, I was thrilled with the opportunity. There was a big budget. The kids were spoiled rotten but well-behaved, and there was a great deal of opportunity for artistic license on my part. I helped select the choral and instrumental music, planned the programs, directed…" She stared off into space for a moment before continuing. "It was a plum job. I was newly graduated, suddenly on my own and living my dream…"

"Sounds perfect," Lance said.

"It was. Anyway, a few years passed, and the head of the department moved on to greener pastures, if such a thing exists, and I was offered his position. Naturally, I accepted. As you know, teaching isn't a well-paid profession. But this gig, what with private lessons and extra-curricular activities on the side, I was pulling down a nice salary. And I loved what I was doing."

"So?"

"It was that first year, when I was director of the music department at St. Andrews, that I met Eric," Olivia paused, her expression troubled. She sighed and continued.

"I'd entered my varsity choir in a competition in the city. They were that good. It was a big deal. We did exceptionally well, placed fourth, but what blew me away was a choir from the inner city. Those kids were amazing. They came from nothing, and quite honestly, this...the music...it was like a lifeline they'd been thrown. That was an epiphany for me, but I didn't realize the implications until much later."

In her mind's eye, Olivia envisioned a large ballroom somewhere in the heart of the city...

It was an elegant affair, and she looked down at herself, knowing full well that she was stunning in her chic, off-the shoulder black cocktail dress. She shook hands with several city officials and local luminaries, a forced smile on her face. Then Eric appeared before her. He was slickly handsome, dashing in his hand-tailored tuxedo. Their eyes met, and he took her arm, drawing her away from the crowd.

Olivia shook her head as she relived that fateful encounter. "Eric swept me off my feet. From the moment I met him, it was as if I no longer had control over my life." She paused, pondering her own words. "Wow. Did I say that? Because that's it...in a nutshell. He just took over. Until there was no more...me."

Suddenly overcome by emotion, Olivia choked back tears while Lance watched helplessly. Moments later, she cleared her throat, composed herself, and continued.

"Eric was like no one I'd ever met. The seduction started immediately, but eventually, the control became the seduction. The changes were incremental. I didn't realize what was happening until one day I was flying high, self-possessed, and free, and in the next, I was little more than a prisoner in my own home." The memory played out like a movie in her head.

Eric sprawled in a lounge chair in his fashionably contemporary living room, intent on the TV screen. The space was dominated by a wall of glass overlooking a panoramic skyline, illuminated by city lights. Olivia saw herself in the sleekly efficient galley kitchen preparing the evening meal. She stirred a saucepan on the cooktop and then reached for a spice jar on the counter.

Eric remained focused on the television. "And cool it with the red pepper flakes, okay?"

Olivia hesitated, holding the spice jar over the pot. "But I prefer it fra diavolo. You know. The way we had it at the Italian restaurant you like so much. You couldn't get enough of it."

"Yeah, well. It gives me indigestion."

Olivia sighed and returned the spice container to the counter. Then she straightened her shoulders and steeled her resolve. "Can we talk?"

"Umm." Eric yawned and stretched, not paying attention.

Olivia turned the burner to low and grabbed a beer from the refrigerator. She poured the contents into a tall glass and sailed around the corner to confront him. "Here you are, darling." She handed him the beer and came to perch before him on the ottoman at his feet.

"Thanks, babe." Eric took a sip of the beverage and set the glass on a coaster on the side table. Then he gave her his full attention. "What's on your mind?"

"I'm seriously thinking about that position in the city."

Eric bolted upright in his chair. "Why the hell would you do that? You've got the perfect job. You love it. You've said so yourself. Besides, I don't want you to work at all once we're married. Let alone in that part of town."

Olivia came to her feet, pivoted, and plopped down on his lap. She draped an arm around his neck. "It's just something I feel I must do. I want to make a difference. The kids at St. Andrews are terrific, but they're privileged; they'd be great with or without me. These kids…they could go one way or the other. And if I turned just one life around…well, I think it would be worth the effort. Don't you?"

Eric took her face in his hands.

Finding the gesture unduly aggressive, Olivia stiffened, but she resisted the impulse to draw away.

"I think there are plenty of others who could step up to that plate. A woman like you…you'd just be asking for trouble. Why won't you let me take care of you?"

Olivia pried Eric's hands away and kissed him lightly on the mouth. "I'm a big girl, Eric. And I just want to give it a go, okay? If it doesn't feel right, or if I feel threatened in any way...I promise I'll give it up." She kissed him again. "Please, back me on this."

Eric's face was stony. "I don't like it, but if that's what you want..."

"Thank you, sweetheart. I'm ready for the challenge, and I just know this is going to be good."

Olivia shook herself from her reverie. "Despite Eric's misgivings, he let me try. And I'm not going to tell you that working with those kids from the inner city was a walk in the park because it wasn't. It was probably the most challenging thing I've ever done in my life. I went from a generous budget to having to buy most of my teaching supplies, the sheet music, CDs, and songbooks. And there were times when I felt as though I was in harm's way. But there were always good kids who watched my back. It was so rewarding. Once I earned their confidence, those students gave me all they had.

"In June, after my first-year teaching there, Eric and I got married. By January, I was pregnant, and he was urging me to quit. My second was a whole lot easier than the first. I was making significant progress with the students, gaining their trust, and I had no intention of leaving them mid-year."

Once again, Olivia found herself back in her classroom in the inner city. Her students stood before her in a semi-circle, holding their sheet music at arm's length. They were a mix of Caucasian, Black, and Hispanic, all good-naturedly unruly.

"Okay, enough already," Olivia cried. "Let's go back to the coda, shall we? Key change, up a half step. Here we go..." She blew on a pitch pipe, motioning for the basses to sing their note, which they did. Then she pointed to the tenors, bringing them in a third higher. She repeated that exercise for the altos and then the sopranos until a rich, full chord resounded.

The spell was broken when one of the bigger boys in the back yelped, "Ouch! Get off my foot, dumb-ass, honky." He shoved the fellow next to him, who subsequently jostled the boy on his other side.

"Don't push me, you freakin' moron," a pimply teen challenged.

Up to this point, the taunts were half in jest, not threatening. But in the next instant, tempers flared, and a melee broke out.

"Get the hell away from me, punk!"

And then the lines of rank formed. Some students egged on the would-be aggressors, eager for confrontation and a diversion. More students hung back, seemingly dismayed by this development. Olivia charged in between the two factions, attempting to quell the impending rumble, and she was followed by a few of those who aspired to do the same.

"Alright, already! Break it up." Olivia muscled her way into the thick of it, and a couple of her students thrust out their hands before them to protect her. Then someone threw a punch. The raised hands deflected the blow, and it glanced off Olivia's shoulder with only a fraction of its intended force. Still, it was enough to put her off balance. As she fell, some of the students rushed in to catch her. Despite their efforts, she hit the floor, and when she did, all the combatants backed away, horrified at this turn of events.

Olivia lay on the tile floor, dazed. A few of the students fell to their knees, surrounding her. One yelled, "Call 911, damn it, and somebody go get the principal."

"It was an accident," another cried, despairingly, as, with horrified eyes, he witnessed the pool of blood seeping from beneath Olivia's skirt. "She slipped and fell, okay? An accident! Do you hear me?"

Olivia fought her way back to the present. She had unburdened a great deal of baggage, and she was a bit numb. Suddenly weepy, she peered blindly out the window, but the scene continued to unspool in her mind.

Lance broke her trance, urging her to continue. "What happened?"

Olivia sighed, fighting back tears. "I lost the baby. Honestly, I don't think the fall had anything to do with it. In my heart of hearts, I believe I would have lost it, anyway. But Eric didn't see it that way. He was furious. He blamed me...said that I was selfish, irresponsible...and so many other hurtful things."

"Insensitive bastard." Lance's eyes smoldered.

Olivia shrugged off his comment. "At the time, his words hit home. I felt incredibly guilty. After all, he'd warned me, and I'd

ignored him. It was almost as if fate had handed me the cards…
that I deserved exactly what I'd gotten."

"You don't believe that."

Olivia turned a tortured face to him. "At the time, I did."

Lance met her eyes. "And now?"

"I don't think that any longer. Now I believe it was a blessing
of sorts. Otherwise, I'd still be with Eric. It took that awful thing to
begin this process. After that, he became even more controlling.
He forbade me to work or do much of anything except tend to his
needs. It was claustrophobic; I couldn't breathe. But when I began
clawing my way out of the postpartum depression and started
feeling more like myself, I realized I had to get away from him,
that there was no possibility of my thriving in that environment.
So, I told him I was going, that I wanted out, and he flew into a
rage. He grabbed my arms and shook me, screaming that I
couldn't leave him. I broke away, and that was the first time he
struck me. It wasn't the last."

"Damn it!"

"There were other incidents, but by then I'd made up my mind.
I bided my time, all the while deceiving him, letting him feel that
he'd won. What I was doing was making plans for my getaway. At
the first opportunity, I ran. The rest you know."

Lance folded his hands on the tabletop before him. "I don't
know what to say. You've had such a horrific time of it. I'm
surprised you've not sworn off men entirely."

"Which is precisely what Annabelle did." Olivia smiled a
small, sad smile. "I will not make that same mistake." She threw
her head back and took a deep breath, and then returned his gaze.
"I realize now that I am so fortunate for having come here, for you
delivering me to Charm. In the short time I've been here, I truly
have begun to heel."

Lance swallowed hard and knuckled moisture from the corner
of his eye. "And I, too, am glad that you landed in our hayfield."

Olivia chuckled. "It's taken me all this time to realize that the
human heart yearns to trust."

"And I let you down."

Olivia shook her head. "You've been a bastion of normal.

You've made me feel…worthy. And you have no idea how attractive, how reassuring, that is."

"I will never let you down again. I promise you that. I care for you, Livy."

Olivia shook her head, so emotionally wrought she was afraid of breaking down entirely.

"Look. I know this is too soon for you. But you might as well know it. I'll wait. Just so long as I can see you…be with you…" Lance took her hand in his. "And when you're ready—"

"Here we go." Charlie swooped in with two coffees and a plate of sugar cookies.

Gently, Olivia drew her hand away from Lance's. "Thanks, Charlie," she said, turning her tear-stained face to the man whom she'd secretly hoped was her father. "Cookies, Charlie? You shouldn't have."

"Nothing but the best for you, dearie!" Charlie regaled, at the same time shooting Lance a warning look.

"Thanks, Charlie," Lance said. The saloon owner's message was loud and clear. "We're good here."

"Damned well better be," Charlie muttered as he moved away.

"Let's just take it slow, okay?" Olivia favored Lance with a watery smile.

"Slow is good," Lance said. "As long as we're moving forward." Then his eyebrows shot up as a thought occurred. "Say, what're you doing tomorrow night?"

Olivia's face brightened, and she couldn't suppress a giggle at Lance's steadfast perseverance.

It was a mere two and a half weeks before Christmas, and nearly all the snow in Crystal Falls had melted. Frozen mounds of slush had been transformed to rime-crusted, brown puddles, and the steady drip, drip, drip of melting icicles was heard everywhere. But this sad state of affairs, the prospect of a snowless Christmas, didn't seem to dampen the children's spirits. They tumbled out of the rehearsal hall and onto the pavement, laughing and shrieking and eager for release.

Lance stood before the row of vehicles parked at the curb, watching as the youngsters streaked past him, searching for their rides.

"Whoo-hoo!" Aiden cried, charging toward the curb.

"Hey there, kid. What's all the excitement?"

The red-headed moppet skidded to a halt before Lance. "I'm a person! Wait till I tell my parents!" Aiden zoomed into the open door of an awaiting SUV, leaving Lance looking mystified.

Soon, all the children had been picked up and whisked away to their respective homes. All, that is, except for a small Latina who was laden with a backpack that seemed far too heavy for her slight frame to bear. But the girl didn't seem to mind that she was the last to be picked up or that the load she carried was burdensome. Humming a Christmas carol, she stamped her tiny feet, beating a rhythm in the sloshy, melting snow.

"Hello, there," Lance called out to her. When she turned to him, Lance caught his breath. The child had the face of an angel! But she did not speak.

"Not supposed to talk to strangers, huh? I get it. Clever girl."

Framed by thick, black lashes, the child's eyes were luminous. She turned away from him, concentrating on the street as if willing a parent to appear.

Lance took in the child's ratty clothing, the too-short sweatpants, the oversized jacket. "I'm waiting for Ms. Olivia," he said. "Just so you know."

The girl turned back to him and smiled. "Ms. Olivia nice."

"Believe me, honey, I think so, too."

A slight, young woman, her head wrapped in a plaid woolen scarf, appeared from around the corner. She scurried toward the girl.

"Ah." The girl raised a hand. "Hola, Mama!"

"Amelie," the woman cried. "Llegue ta rapido como pude." *I came as soon as I could.*

"Esta Bien, Mama. No he esperado mucho." *I didn't wait long.*

"How do you do, Ma'am?" Lance said.

"Hello." The woman turned her attention to Lance, a guarded look in her eyes. "Amelie not bother you?"

"Oh, no." Lance shook his head vehemently. "She was perfect. Refused to speak to me, as a matter of fact." He touched a finger to his lips and shook his head.

"Amelie…" The woman frowned at her daughter.

"Which was a very good thing," Lance rushed to explain. "You've taught her well." He pinched his thumb and index finger together and then brought them to his lips. "She *shouldn't* speak to strangers, and that's a fact."

Suddenly, the door to the hall opened, and Olivia's bell-like laugh rang out. She and Rhett, guitar cases in hand, emerged from the building, their heads together. Once outside, Olivia pivoted to lock the door. When she drew away and turned toward the street, she spied the threesome on the curb.

"Lance, I didn't expect you!" She hurried toward him. "And Amelie. Is this your mother?"

"Yes," the small girl said, her dark eyes round as saucers.

Olivia closed the distance between them. "Hello! Mrs. García, is it?"

"Gabriella, Si. Yes, ma'am," the woman replied in broken English.

"I'm very pleased to make your acquaintance. I want to thank you for allowing your daughter to sing in the pageant."

"I get off work now," the woman admitted. "Para hacer honesta." *It's a convenience.*

"Lucky for us," Oliva said. "Amelie has a lovely voice. But I'm sure you're already aware of that."

"Oh, yes." Mrs. García beamed at her daughter. "She sing all the time with TV, the radio. Always sing. Her Papá say she his canarito."

"I'll have you know your little canary will be playing the part of Mary in our nativity scene." Olivia grinned as she delivered this news.

Mrs. García gasped and took a step back. "Gracias, Miss. Is an honor."

Rhett came to stand behind Olivia. "Yes, it is," he said. "But your girl's gifted. She deserves a chance."

"If you don't mind," Olivia said. "I'd like to give her some voice lessons. No charge, of course."

Gabriella put a hand to her chest. "That would be…" She struggled for the words in English, but they would not come. "Que bendición," she said. "¡Muchas Gracias!"

"Good. Then that's settled." Olivia hunkered down, coming eye to eye with Amelie, and wrinkled her nose. "Now, home with you, little canary. And don't overdo it with the singing. You've got to keep that voice of yours in shape for the pageant."

Amelie and her mother smiled their thanks and turned away.

"Wow," Lance breathed, his eyes following the beautiful child and her mother as they made their way down the street. "You just never know, do you?"

"No," Olivia agreed. "Her family's been in Crystal Falls for less than a year. God knows the hardships they endured coming here, fleeing Guatemala with only the clothes on their backs. The church is sponsoring them. Amelie has an older brother, you see. He was being coerced into joining a gang, and…"

"Oh, hell," Lance muttered.

"They're not legal. But the church is helping them navigate the system. With a little assistance and a lot of luck, they'll assimilate."

"I'm not an immigration attorney, but perhaps I could do something to help them out."

Olivia shot Lance a grateful smile. "That would be wonderful."

"Gorgeous girl," Rhett said. "Talented, too."

"Well." Lance focused on Olivia. "I thought maybe we could have a nightcap." He turned and looked hard at Rhett, hoping the oversized windbag would graciously bow out.

Instead, Rhett said, "Great idea! I could do with a brew."

Lance rolled his eyes, and then he turned back to Olivia. "What do you say?"

"Fine by me."

"Nesbitt's?"

"Where else?"

The three set off down the street, Lance on Olivia's right, Rhett on her left, both men with guitar cases slung over their broad shoulders.

Rhett pushed open the door of the pub, and the threesome clamored in, snickering at some lame joke he'd cracked. All the booths were occupied. After a quick look around, they made a beeline to an empty four-top in the back of the pub and began shedding their outerwear.

Although the dining room was nearly full, only a few patrons sat at the bar. Charlie breezed out from the kitchen, took one look at Olivia and her two escorts, and did a doubletake.

He grabbed three menus and then strode to their table. "One's not enough for you, huh, sweetheart?"

Charlie winked at Olivia as though they shared some secret, and Olivia couldn't help but laugh. She knew it was absurd, but she felt safe in the company of these three very disparate men.

Rhett guffawed good-naturedly at the bar owner's suggestive comment, but Lance merely looked glum.

"I'll have you know, Mr. Nesbitt," Olivia said. "I was told by a local authority, mind you, that these two prime specimens are the most eligible bachelors in Crystal Falls County."

"Madam," Charlie bowed slightly at the waist. "You were not misinformed. Need a menu, or do you know what you *want?*" He looked pointedly at Olivia, an impish grin on his face, and it was apparent he was not speaking of menu items.

Olivia shot him a sugary smile, pretending not to get the gist of his comment. "I want something *hot*. How about an Irish coffee?"

"Warm the cockles of your heart?"

"Make mine a Guinness," Rhett said.

"Stout!" Charlie cried.

"Chavis on ice," Lance said.

"Regal," Charlie shot back.

The mood lightened and they all chuckled, and then Charlie crossed to the bar.

"So, how's the pageant shaping up?" Lance asked.

"Very well." Olivia turned to her partner in song, naked admiration in her eyes. "Rhett's written some fabulous new material, and he's agreed to debut his compositions at the pageant." She swiveled to face Lance. "Isn't that special?"

Rhett shrugged away the compliment, and Lance raised his eyebrows. "Impressive."

"The kids are so darn cute," Rhett said. "Doesn't matter whether they mess up or not; they'll be a hit in any case."

"Say, I ran into Aiden McGill." Lance eyed Olivia. "Or, rather, he ran into me. The boy was all wound up. Said he was a person. What's that all about?"

Olivia chuckled. "It means he's not a star or an animal. He's got a speaking part."

Just then, Charlie arrived with their drinks order. "Here you go." He set their glasses down. "And this is for the lady." He placed a large basket on the table. "Homemade potato chips, on the house."

"Yummy," Olivia gushed. "Thanks, Charlie."

"Where are the usual suspects, Charlie?" Rhett glanced at the nearly empty bar and then reached for a chip. "It's awfully quiet around here tonight."

The tavern keeper put a finger to his lips. "Got us a poker game in the back, but you didn't hear it from me. Wouldn't want to get busted or nothing. Of course, the fact that the sheriff is winning might preclude that from happening."

"I thought the poker game was at Timmy Corker's," Lance said, munching on a chip.

"Change of plans," Charlie said. "Lizzy Corker's book club was having a meeting there. And that took precedence, don't you know?"

In the next moment, the front door burst open, and like an ill wind, a stranger in a long dark coat over black trousers stormed in. He ripped the sunglasses from off his face, his head swinging from side to side as he scanned the room, crying, "Where is she?"

At the sound of his ornery bellow, every conversation ceased, and all eyes turned to the malcontent who'd have been deemed handsome had it not been for the evil sneer on his face.

Shrinking in her seat, Olivia's formerly cheerful expression was transformed to a mask of horror.

It took but an instant for Eric to ferret her out and to take note of the two men accompanying her. Like a bull at Pamplona, he lowered his head, preparing to charge.

"Uh oh," Rhett muttered as Eric steamed toward their booth. "This joker's looking for trouble."

Out of the corner of her eye, Olivia noted that Lance was sizing up the madman suddenly hovering over them, and the light of recognition dawning in his eyes was impossible to miss. She saw, too, that Rhett appeared puzzled but ready for action.

"We need to talk." Ignoring the men, Eric glowered at Olivia.

"You shouldn't have come here," Olivia said, her voice low and firm. "I have nothing to say to you, Eric." She struggled to present an unruffled demeanor, but under the table, she wrung the napkin on her lap.

Deliberately unhurried, Lance unfolded himself from the booth and rose to his full height, and Rhett gained his legs beside him. At six-foot-three, Lance was a good two inches taller than Eric. A gym rat and well-muscled, Rhett had about twenty pounds on him. The imposing pair presented a united front.

"Look at you. It didn't take you long, you slu…"

Lance lunged for Eric, but Rhett held him back. Still, Lance's face was inches from that of the interloper. "Shut your filthy mouth." He renewed his efforts to get at Eric, but Rhett continued to restrain him.

Wolflike, Eric bared his teeth.

"Eric!" Olivia jumped to her feet. "Stop!"

"It appears the *lady* is not interested in anything you have to say." Rhett put his face in Eric's.

At that moment, Chester sauntered in from the back room. "Charlie, what's holding up those dri…" Bewildered, Chester's words died in his throat as he looked from Charlie to Olivia and her companions, to the stranger who appeared to be itching for a fight. Slowly, he nodded his head. Then he turned to the open doorway. "Come out here, fellows." He gestured for the men in the backroom to come and join him.

Charlie Nesbitt had been slinging drinks long enough to know when a potential confrontation required defusing. Deftly, he insinuated himself between Lance and Eric. "Okay, boys," he said. "Break it up."

Chester crossed down to the scene of the altercation and was soon joined by Timmy, Les, and the Crawford brothers, some with drinks still in hand. At the same time, two burly, uniformed state troopers entered the pub and crossed to stand behind Eric.

The sheriff puffed out his chest, planted his feet, and put a hand on his side holster. "Appears as though we've got us a sit-u-a-tion." He tipped his hat at the state troopers. "Howdy, boys. What can we do for you?"

"You can get out of my way," Eric snarled. "I'm here for my wife."

Chester took this information in stride, turned, and peered sanguinely at the trooper's badges. Then he took a step backward and crossed his arms over his chest. "Hmm," he mused. "Kinda outta your jurisdiction, aren't you, fellas? Let me see…that would be…uh…Mickey Duggan? He's your chief. Am I right?"

The cops nodded, seeming both impressed and chastened.

"Yep. That's what I thought. Listen, you boys best stay out of this. We don't want no trouble."

"That woman's my wife." Eric jabbed a finger in Olivia's direction. "And she's coming with me."

Again, Lance lunged at Eric, and again Rhett held him back.

"Like hell she is!" Lance spat.

"She's depressed," Eric said. "Not in her right mind." He swept open his long coat, withdrew an envelope from an inside pocket, and held it before him. "I'm having her Baker Acted. Here's the paperwork. It's for her own good."

"Not in my county, you're not," Chester shot back. "That woman's probably the most level-headed female I ever met in my life."

"Look, Gomer. She's my wife. You can't stop me."

"Oh, but I can," Chester said, a grim smile on his face.

"You don't seem to understand. I'm having her committed."

Olivia's eyes grew wide at this information. Even she could not believe the depths to which Eric would go to have his way.

"What is the matter with you?" she screeched.

Suddenly, seemingly out of nowhere, Cee-Cee appeared next to her. She wrapped an arm around Olivia's quacking shoulder and whispered in her ear. "I've got you, girl. It's going to be okay."

"The only committing that's going to happen here is *you* to the county jail." Chester thrust a finger at Eric's chest. "Lest you cease and desist, my friend."

Lance, further incensed by Eric's declaration, was still struggling against Rhett's tree-trunk arms. He inched toward Eric by degrees.

Eric flinched. "Get away from me!"

Timmy saw the punch coming and tried to warn him. "Lance, watch out!"

But it was too late. Before Lance could react, Eric threw a sucker punch in his direction, and with Rhett restraining him, he was powerless to avoid the blow. It landed squarely on his nose. Blood spurted from his nostrils and poured down his face, and he bent at the waist, reeling from the impact.

"Oh, no." Rhett roared. "No, you don't!" He released Lance, drew back a fist the size of a small capon, and slugged Eric smack in the jaw.

A rounder!

Eric fell back into the arms of one of the police officers. The cop beside him looked baffled, uncertain how to proceed.

In the next instant, Eric wrested free. He wanted a fight. But was it with Lance or Rhett? He didn't seem to know.

"Take it outside, boys," Charlie cautioned.

Vince crossed to Lance, snagged a paper napkin off the table, and pressed it to his son's nose. Lance snatched the napkin from his hand, swiped at his bloody nose, and then tossed it aside. Dog-like, he shook his head as if to clear it.

Vince retreated a few steps, coming to stand next to Rudy. Talking out of the side of his face in a stage whisper, he said, "Fifty bucks says Lance takes him."

Rudy narrowed his eyes and took stock of Eric. "You're on," he breathed.

"Outside is fine by me," Eric scoffed. "But I want a fair fight." He shrugged out of his coat, letting it fall to the floor. "I'll gladly have a go at both of you, but one at a time."

Rhett looked at Lance, clearly ready to follow his lead, but Lance was focused on Eric and already moving. Rudely, Lance brushed past him, intentionally jostling him as he strode across the room toward the entrance.

Enraged, he spat between clenched teeth, "That won't be necessary."

"Lance, don't," Olivia wailed as Cee-Cee held her tightly.

Far past reason, Lance ignored her.

He exploded out the door.

THIRTEEN
DOWN FOR THE COUNT

I t was smack dab in the middle of Main Street where Lance and Eric faced off. All of Charlie's other patrons, the diners, the drinkers, and the gamblers, had surged outside to view the spectacle, calling out words of encouragement to Lance.

Slowly, Eric unknotted the silk tie about his neck, slipped it off, and then handed it to one of the cops. Then he rolled up his shirt sleeves and sneered at Lance.

"Show 'em what you got, Lance!" Vince cried.

"Pretty city boy, he's no match for you, Lance," Timmy hollered.

Eric wove and bobbed, displaying some former training in the ring. Lance was less skilled but more powerful. He kept his fists up and managed to avoid Eric's first few jabs. But then Eric caught him with a glancing wallop to the jaw. Lance staggered but kept his feet. Mulishly, he endured Eric's pummeling, waiting for an opening.

It was painful to watch the beating Lance was taking. Olivia cringed at each blow that found its mark. Eric threw yet another punch, but Lance wove and dodged the fist rocketing toward him, and that provided the moment he'd been waiting for. He drew back his right arm and, concentrating all his energy, crashed his knuckles into his opponent's forehead. Eric's head whipped back.

Unseeing, his corneas retreated to his cerebellum. Then he hit the pavement.

He was out cold.

Lance, his shirt torn, his well-defined pecs heaving as blood coursed down his face, swayed over his fallen adversary. Olivia and Rhett rushed to him while Chester and the two policemen crossed to stand near the defeated pugilist.

Lance collapsed to his knees.

"Lance, are you hurt?" Olivia reached out to touch his battered face, but he jerked away, and, instead, she rummaged through the contents of her purse for a tissue. "Oh, my God!" she castigated herself as she dabbed at his wounds. "I was afraid something like this would happen."

"Ugh." Lance turned his head and spat blood. "I'm fine."

Rhett put a hand under Lance's arm and hauled him to his feet. "Hey, partner. You didn't leave me a shot at the sonofaB."

Lance managed a crooked smile.

Rudy upended his glass and tipped the ice dregs into a handkerchief. Then he and Vince crossed to Lance.

"You did good, son," Rudy said, pressing the makeshift icepack to his nephew's battered nose. "Cost me fifty bucks, but that's okay."

"You all right, son?" Vince asked.

Lance nodded. "Never better."

Chester stood before the two state troopers. "You best bundle your friend into your paddy wagon and vamoose out of here, fellas. But before you leave, I need to get clear on an important detail."

One officer, still kneeling by the unconscious Barone, adjusted his stance to focus on the sheriff, while the other stood respectfully before Chester, giving him his undivided attention.

"I ask you; is it necessary for me to give Mick Duggan a call?'

One of the troopers said, "No sir. We're good, sir."

The other shook his head. "Just a little misunderstanding, is all."

"Well, understand this." Chester rocked on his heels. "As far as I'm concerned, it never happened. Does that work for you boys?"

"Absolutely, sir."

The officers dragged Eric to his feet. By this time, Les, Timmy, and Charlie had lined up behind Chester, while Olivia, Rhett, Rudy, and Vince surrounded Lance, and all the other patrons crowded around. It was an impressive show of solidarity, and the meaning was not lost on the highway troopers.

"One more thing," Chester called, and the policemen turned to face him. "When that..." He pointed to Eric. "Whew, boy! Words fail me. When that...miserable excuse comes to...? You tell him, *this is done*." Chester looked pointedly to Olivia for confirmation.

"It's done," she agreed. She turned to search Lance's gaze.

He gave an almost imperceptible nod of his head, which was all he could muster, given the circumstances.

Chester looked around at the men and women of Crystal Falls, each of whom signaled their approval. "Olivia has people here," he said. "She's dug in. And we stand by our own. You got that?"

The cops nodded and then manhandled Eric toward one of their vehicles.

Olivia pursed her lips, fighting back tears as a heaviness gathered in the back of her throat.

Cee-Cee patted her gently on the back.

Charlie crossed to the door of the pub and opened it. "Woo-he, boy! What a night," he crowed. "Come on in, everybody. Drinks on the house!"

There was much hooting and laughter as the small crowd surged toward the pub.

"Come on. Let's go inside," Cee-Cee said to Olivia. "It's freezing out here."

Only then did Olivia feel the cold. Still, she hung back. "You go on ahead. I'll be in in a minute."

Cee-Cee looked from Olivia to Lance, and then, giving a slight shake of her head, she left Olivia's side to join the others heading for the entryway.

Olivia's gaze went first to Lance and then came to rest on Rhett, and a silent communication passed between them.

Rhett crossed to her, favoring her with a small, sad smile. "It's okay, Livy," he murmured, his voice barely audible. "The best man won."

Olivia responded by giving him a brief hug.

The threesome slowly made their way back to the tavern, Rhett and Olivia on either side of Lance, supporting him as they went.

An hour later, the party was in full swing, many glasses having been raised and pints downed. There was a great deal of ribald laughter and clapping of backs at the retelling of the tale that would become part of the Crystal Falls history. Lance had cleaned up some, and there was a bandage across the bridge of his nose and another over his left eye. He and Olivia sat in their favorite booth by the window, this time shoulder to shoulder rather than across from one another.

Outside, it had begun to snow, large heavy flakes illuminated by a thousand Christmas lights, silently falling from an opaque sky. Olivia's eyes shone as she looked out at the streets of Crystal Falls, which were now being blanketed in a pristine white coverlet.

"It's so beautiful," she said, patting Lance on his rock-hard quadricep.

It was an intimate gesture and one that was not lost on Lance. Clasping her hand in his, he brought it to his lips and nuzzled her knuckles. "You're so beautiful."

"So much trouble, you mean."

"In the words of Theodore Roosevelt, *Nothing in the world is worth having…unless it means effort, pain…difficulty…*"

"Then you've surely paid the price." Olivia chuckled humorlessly.

"And you're surely worth it."

One week before Christmas, Main Street was thronged with holiday shoppers bundled against the cold. Olivia trotted down the sidewalk and then turned onto Adams. Here the street was far less crowded, and it didn't take her long to locate the address she was searching for. Not surprisingly, it was an impressive two-story red brick edifice, and she paused before the building to admire it. With its sturdy, Corinthian-capped columns, and dental molding, it exuded a sense of permanence and money. A tasteful sign in black lettering edged in gold proclaimed *T.C. Enterprises*.

Olivia's high-heeled boots made a clicking sound as she traversed the travertine floor and made her way down the hallway. She stopped before a paneled mahogany door, took a deep breath, and knocked before entering. Inside, the office suite was beautifully appointed with luxurious Wilton carpets, gilt-framed oil paintings, and brass and crystal chandeliers. The receptionist, a severe-looking young woman, sat at an antique French desk embellished with gold ormolu.

Olivia squared her shoulders and approached her. "Olivia Barone," she said. "I'm here to see Mr. Corker."

"Yes, Ms. Barone. He's expecting you." The receptionist rose and escorted Olivia to Timmy's posh private office. "T.C., Ms. Barone to see you."

Timmy, a compact man behind a behemoth of a desk, bolted to his feet, and in this opulent setting, his bigger-than-life personality somehow seemed proportionate.

He beamed, extending a hand to Olivia.

The receptionist turned on her heel and exited.

"Livy, what a pleasure." Timmy took Olivia's hand in his.

Standing before him, the enormity of what she was about to reveal struck her, and Olivia's smile crumpled.

Watching the emotions play over Olivia's face, Timmy's sunny countenance clouded. "Olivia, what is it? What's the matter, dear?"

Olivia pressed a knuckle to her eye and wrested control of her emotions. "I'm sorry. I seem to be saying that a lot lately. Sorry, sorry." She screwed up her face and managed a self-deprecating chuckle.

Timmy patted her shoulder and then escorted her to a chair beside his desk. "There, there," he said, hovering over her solicitously. "You've been through a lot. I'm only beginning to realize just how much. It's okay. Think nothing of it. You and Lance... why, you were magnificent last night. It was really something." He shook his head, recalling the recent events at the tavern. Stepping back apace, he beamed at her. "Now, what can I do for you?"

"I'm afraid that what I have to say might come as a shock." Olivia dug in her bag and withdrew the old photograph.

"I don't scare easily," Timmy said.

"It's not much to go on, I know," Olivia continued. "But my mother was very secretive..."

Olivia handed the photograph to Timmy, and he stared up at her, confused.

"I think you may be my father."

Timmy's face drained of color. He took the proffered photograph and staggered behind his desk. There, he collapsed into his desk chair, and looking stunned, gazed at the photograph.

Olivia gave him a moment to compose himself, and then she pushed on. "That was your house, wasn't it?"

The stocky fellow took a deep breath and then slowly exhaled. "Yes, it was, but..."

"And that's you with my mother. Isn't it?"

"Your mother?" Timmy gazed at the photograph. Then he eyed Olivia. "Oh!" His jaw dropped and he sat back heavily in his chair. It took him several moments to speak. When he did, the words came tumbling out in a rush.

"I can't believe it! I knew you looked familiar." His face took on a look of regret. "I hate to disappoint you, dear, but that's not me in the photo."

Olivia's hands flew to her mouth. "What do you mean? It's your house."

Timmy bolted up from his chair and crossed to the dark walnut bookcase that dominated one wall. He searched for a volume, quickly located it, and thumbed through the pages. "There." He thrust the album toward Olivia. "See. Same house. Same girl. But that guy is not me."

Olivia peered at the photograph. It was identical to the one she'd brought, except that the man seated next to her mother was thinner and taller than the fellow in her photo. And, unlike

Olivia's photograph, the young man in Timmy's photo was more sharply defined. Olivia was thunderstruck. Clearly, it was Charlie Nesbitt.

Charlie was her father!

Timmy crossed to a small sofa on the far wall and seated himself with the album on his lap. Then he patted the seat cushion next to him. "You're as white as a sheet. Come sit here, and I'll explain."

Olivia went to sit beside him, and Timmy turned to the next page of the album, tore out a photo, and handed it to Olivia. "Look."

Olivia looked first at the photo and then back at the album, where multiple variations of the image were displayed.

"It was my birthday, you see. My folks gave me a Polaroid and some film. It was a big splurge for them. Naturally, I couldn't wait to take some pictures of myself with my best friends. We took turns snapping pics of each other."

He looked away, recalling that long-lost time of innocence before resuming. Then he turned to her. "How much do you know about your mother's upbringing?"

"Very little. She didn't talk much about her past."

"Hmm…" Timmy took a deep breath and then continued. "That summer, we were the Three Musketeers, Charlie, Naomi, and me. Your great aunt and uncle were very strict; they didn't appreciate having young people underfoot. Poor as church mice, my parents were generous souls. Charlie's family was even worse off than mine; he had it pretty rough. Me? My folks were easy-going, laid back. What were a few more kids, huh? So, more often than not, we hung out at my place.

"Practically from the first time he laid eyes on her, Charlie was besotted by your mother. Oh, I had a crush on her, too. You bet! But Naomi was the sun and moon to Charlie. And it was plain to see, she felt the same about him."

Timmy snapped his fingers, swiveling in his chair to favor Olivia with a small smile. "You're the spitting image of your mother. It's a wonder Charlie didn't see it. How is she?"

"She passed away eight months ago."

"I'm sorry." Timmy sobered. "That's a shame. She was a lovely girl. So good-natured and full of life…"

"That's not how I remember her."

"Sometimes circumstances change people." Timmy shook his head as memories flooded his brain. "Believe me. She was." Then he shifted the album to Olivia's lap and came to his feet. "How about a beverage? A Coke? A glass of water? Or something stronger?"

"Water would be wonderful."

Timmy crossed to a small credenza housing a mini fridge. From it he withdrew a bottle of water, which he proceeded to divide between two crystal glasses, "Say, I hope you're not too disappointed, Olivia." He crossed the distance between them. "It'd tickle me pink to learn that I was your daddy." Handing her a glass and then resuming his seat beside her. "Liz and I always wanted a passel of kids. Sad to say, that wasn't in the cards for us. But now, I think you should be calling me Uncle Tim."

Olivia sagged against the entrepreneur's shoulder, and they both stared down at the photographs. Suddenly, an idea sparked, and Timmy whistled. "Boy, oh boy!" He reached over to cover Olivia's hand with his. "Old Charlie is in for a surprise, huh?"

Olivia pulled a face at the thought, but in the next instant, she was laughing. "That he is, Uncle Tim. That he is."

Back in her private suite at Charm, Olivia sat before her dressing table mirror carefully touching up her makeup. Weariness crashed over her. Given the encounter with Timmy this afternoon, she was emotionally drained. But she willed herself to rally. She needed to be at the church hall for a pageant rehearsal in a little over an hour. After that, there was one more task she needed to attend to before the day was out.

There'd been so much emotional baggage for her to process in so short a time. Now, despite her fatigue, Olivia felt strangely empowered, ready to expunge the past and embrace a future that seemed full of exciting possibilities.

"I was right to come here, Milo," she murmured.

From his vantage point atop the bed, the little terrier raised his silvery head and rewarded her with a doggie affirmative, a resounding yip.

"I'm glad you agree."

※

It was a bitterly cold night, the velvet sky pierced by myriad pinpricks of light. Olivia's breath billowed in a white cloud before her as she noted the icicles fanging from the manor's eaves. Milo, on a leash, scrambled ahead, seemingly eager to return to the warmth of their room.

Having come from the backyard, she was just gaining the sidewalk, when a familiar voice rang out. "Hello, there!"

"Cee-Cee!" Olivia exclaimed, upon catching sight of the Black woman. She was bundled in a puffy jacket with a faux fur-lined hood framing her pretty face. "What are you doing?"

Startled, Milo barked a greeting only to have it returned by a luxuriously coated Pomeranian, whom Cee-Cee was walking. Tails wagging, the two dogs whined happily and touched noses.

Celia snickered. "Same as you, it seems. Getting in one last pee of the day." She gestured vaguely to her right. "I'm just two blocks down from here, on Drayton. It's not on the other side of the tracks, but it's surely not so grand a street as this one. I love walking here. Anyway, I guess you could say we're neighbors."

Olivia hunkered down to pat the Pom on its tan head. "And who is this gorgeous creature?"

"This is Bella."

"She's beautiful." Olivia stood and stepped toward Celia, meeting her gaze. "Thank you for your support the other night. It was good that you were there. But afterward, there was such chaos inside, that by the time I had the presence of mind to try and find you—"

"I'd gone."

"Yeah. I'm sorry."

"No apologies necessary. You had a lot going on."

Olivia laughed." That's an understatement! Hey, I've got to leave in twenty minutes for a rehearsal, but would you like to come in for a quick peek around?"

"Are you kidding? I've been dying to see the inside of this place for as long as I can remember."

Fifteen minutes later they were back outside, Olivia stowing her guitar and satchel in the backseat of the BMW, Cee-Cee with Bella in tow.

"So, it's all turned out okay then?" Celia asked.

"Who knows?" Olivia sighed. "Like I said, it went really well with Timmy. Not as I'd anticipated, but well." She closed the back passenger door and turned to her friend. "We'll see how I make out with Charlie."

Cee-Cee leaned in to bestow an awkward, one-armed hug to Olivia. "He's a sweetie," she said drawing away. "Trust me; it'll be fine. At least now I know why you were so aghast when I suggested that your dad might be a Crawford."

"Mmhmm." Olivia said. "*That's* complicated enough as it is."

"Relax, Olivia," Celia said. "Don't overthink this. Just have fun and enjoy the attentions of a wonderful man."

"I'm trying, but it's harder than you think. And what about you, huh? Where's your Mr. Right?"

"I don't know, honey. It's been a long dry spell."

"Well, he's out there. It's only a matter of time. Mark my words."

It was after eleven, and Charlie had locked up the tavern and retired to his rooms. He was dozing in his leather recliner, a football game airing on his muted, flat-screen TV. In one corner, a small, table-top Christmas tree, with colored lights and shiny ornaments, lent holiday cheer to the otherwise spartan interior. Alley Cat lay curled in an orange and black stripe at his feet.

When the doorbell rang, Charlie opened his eyes wide, and the tabby's head shot up, ears pricked.

"Who could that be?" he muttered. Charlie roused himself, yawned, and crossed to the door only to find Olivia standing outside on the landing.

"Livy! For crying out loud, what are you doing here at this time of night? Come on in, girl. It's freezing out there."

"I hope it's not too late." Olivia stood on the threshold. "We were rehearsing for the pageant. I dismissed the kids hours ago, but Rhett and I stayed on. When we finally called it quits, I happened to see your light on." She shrugged. "I thought I'd chance it. I hope I'm not inconveniencing you."

"No, not at all." He motioned for her to come inside, and Olivia complied. Charlie closed the door behind her. "Have a seat."

Olivia unbuttoned her coat and settled herself in an upholstered chair, and Charlie came to stand before her. "Can I get you something? Coffee? Hot cocoa? A whiskey?"

"No, thanks. I won't keep you long."

Charlie scooped up Alley and resumed his seat. He stroked the cat, a puzzled expression on his face. "I can't help but wonder to what it is I owe this pleasure."

Olivia withdrew the folded paper and the photograph from her handbag. Then she leaned forward and handed him the letter.

"What's this?" Charlie searched her eyes.

"Read it." Olivia watched as Charlie poured over the letter, desperately trying to gauge his reaction.

As he read, Charlie's brow furrowed. When he finished, he looked up. "Where did you get this?"

Olivia was silent, waiting for him to come to the inevitable conclusion. It took only a few moments before he wrapped his head around the obvious. Dumbfounded, his jaw slackened, and he clapped a palm to his forehead.

Olivia shot him a tentative smile. Then she held out the photograph. "I never knew who my real father was. Mom kept it a big mystery till the very end."

Charlie grasped the photo and gazed at it, seemingly transfixed.

"When she passed away…"

Charlie cut his gaze to Olivia's.

"She died a few months ago."

"I'm terribly sorry to hear that," he said, his voice suddenly thick with emotion. His gaze shifted to the framed photograph of Naomi on the side table and then back to Olivia.

"Yeah. Anyway, I came across the letter and photograph while sorting through her things. I found them pressed between the pages of an anthology of Shakespeare's plays. And Timmy gave me that one."

Charlie shook his head and smiled. "Your mom had a thing for Shakespeare. She was smart as a whip." He bounded to his feet. "Oh, Livy!" He extended his arms, and Olivia vaulted out of her chair and fell into them. Charlie embraced her, stroking her hair. Then he held her at arm's length. "I should have seen it," he said, searching her face. "You look so much like her, my beautiful Naomi."

"What happened?"

Charlie sighed, letting his arms drop to his side. Then he collapsed back into his recliner, and Olivia resumed her seat. "Well, as I'm sure you figured out by the letter, I got her in trouble. But I loved her. I wanted to marry her. I begged her to tell her folks, but she was afraid to. And she refused to run off with me. Which, in hindsight, was probably for the best. Young people can be very foolish and headstrong." Charlie bit his lower lip, lost in the past. Then he continued.

"She simply vanished. This was before the Internet. You couldn't just Google someone. I never knew what became of her, and not for lack of trying. All I could figure was that your grand-parents sent her off somewhere. Shortly after that, they moved away, and I never heard from her again. I always thought she'd get in touch with me, but she never did. I was still in love with her, but there was nothing to be done. So, I enlisted in the Marines. I came back here when I completed my tour, bought a dilapidated saloon, and fixed her up. The rest is history. The years just flew by.

Maybe she did try to contact me while I was overseas. Now I'll never know."

"It's so sad," Olivia sniffed. "What might have been…"

"Yeah," Charlie agreed, looking heartbroken. But, in the next moment, his spirits soared. "Hey, no long faces here! We got us a happy ending after all. Don't we?" he crowed. "I got me a talented, gorgeous daughter. And you…why I guess you got the booby prize."

Olivia grinned. "Nah! I couldn't be happier." Her heart seemed to expand in her chest as an irrepressible joy washed over her. She crossed to Charlie and lowered herself down to perch on the arm of his chair. "Oh, Dad! May I call you that?"

Charlie snaked an arm around her waist. "I sure do like the sound of it, honey."

FOURTEEN
THE PAGEANT

Christmas was four days away, and the church hall was awash in red and white poinsettias. Olivia stood center stage, surrounded by children. Others were either seated in folding chairs before the stage or tearing up and down the aisles. Some were dressed in costume, but most were in street clothes. Mrs. Ellis pounded the organ. Rhett strummed his guitar to a different melody.

It was mass pandemonium.

Olivia blew on the whistle attached to a cord around her neck, and the children quieted. "Okay," she cried. "All kids on stage now. I mean it. Hurry up! We've got a lot to accomplish tonight, so I need everyone to pay attention."

A child squealed, and Olivia blew another blast on her whistle. "All right. We're going to rehearse from the last performance to the first. That means we're going backward." At this news, there were groans from the children.

"It's a good practice. You'll see. We start with the nativity scene. Mary, Joseph, and Innkeeper, I want you here." Olivia pointed to where each of the main characters was to stand, and Amelie and the boy playing Joseph found their marks.

"Narrator, you're here." Olivia looked around, but no narrator appeared. "Where is he?"

"Aiden," one of the youngsters yelled.

"Aiden McGill!" another cried.

"Here! I'm coming." Aiden scrambled up the side stairs to the stage.

"Mr. McGill, you asked to be a person. Isn't that right?"

"Yes, Ms. Olivia."

"Well then, I expect you to keep your ears open and to be on stage when you're supposed to be."

"Yes, ma'am." Aiden scooted front and center.

"Good. Wise men upstage. No," Olivia motioned. "That side. Remember. My right is your left. Shepherds and sheep, stage left. Angels and stars, up-center. Narrator, that's you, Aiden. Move down-center. That's right, closer to the audience. Okay. Now, look where you are, people. These are your *places*. When I call *places*, this is where you go."

Suddenly, one of the teenage boys belched loudly, and the children erupted in hoots and giggles.

"Oh, brother," Olivia muttered before screeching, "Quiet!" at the top of her lungs. Then, except for a few coughs and one stifled sneeze, the children were silent, giving her their undivided attention.

"Anne, Rhett?" Olivia motioned for the accompaniment to begin, and in the next instant, the calypso beat of *LONG TIME AGO IN BETHLEHEM* filled the air with a sultry, island melody.

Three hours and forty-five minutes later, the children had been dismissed. Only Rhett and Olivia remained on stage. Seated on stools, they faced one another while singing the final verse of Rhett's original *CHRISTMAS IN THE COUNTRY.*

As they did so, and unbeknownst to them, Lance pushed open the double doors and entered the foyer, only to be enveloped in a sweet melody. Making as little noise as possible, he crept into the main hall and leaned against a column in the back. He was riveted.

Rhett sang:

"At Christmastime, you'll find me."

Olivia sang the next line:

"Where the love-light shines."

Rhett bobbed his head in time to the beat.

"Can happen anytime."

Olivia echoed:

"Anytime."
"You believe."

They finished together:

"Why would you…"
Ever leave?"

Then, as Rhett continued playing, Olivia picked up a set of sleigh bells by her feet and shook them in time to the beat.

Ching, ching, ching, ching,
Ching, ching, ching, ching, CHING!

At the song's end, Lance applauded, loud and slow, while making his way to the stage.

Olivia's head snapped up. "Lance!"

"You guys are *really good*," Lance said, the admiration in his voice hard to miss. "Did you write that, Rhett? It's fantastic!"

"Thank you, my man. Livy has pushed me to record a Christmas album. Something I would never have done if it weren't for this silly pageant. So…as Annabelle always says, everything—

"…happens for a reason," Lance and Olivia finished his sentence, and they all laughed.

"You're going to make it big time, Rhett," Lance said, clapping

Rhett on the back. "I believe this..." He pointed his chin at the sheet music on a stand before Rhett and Olivia. "This is your ticket."

"Ah, we'll see." Rhett brushed off the compliment. Then, snatching up the sheet music, he and Olivia clambered down the side steps and began packing up their guitars.

"I agree," Olivia said, turning toward Rhett. "I honestly believe you've got a chance at landing a major record deal. It's all about timing, isn't that so?"

"It'd be awfully nice to make a few bucks for a change," Rhett admitted. "Don't get me wrong; I love spinning tunes for a local radio station, but that's not to say I'm bringing home the big bucks."

He donned his coat and hastened toward the entrance while Olivia and Lance hung back.

"I've got to run, kids." Rhett paused before exiting the hall. "I have to be in the studio bright and early."

"Good night, Rhett," Olivia called to him.

"See ya," Rhett cried out from the foyer. In the next moment, he'd levered a door open and disappeared into the snowy night.

"That man is so much bigger than life," Olivia said, once she and Lance were alone. "I swear, it's exhausting being in his presence."

Lance wrapped his arms around Olivia, drawing her to him, and she let her satchel drop to the floor and surrendered to their first kiss.

It went on and on.

"Do I exhaust you?" Lance murmured when, at last, they slowly drew apart.

"Oh, my," Olivia murmured breathlessly. "Not at all. Quite the opposite, in fact..." She draped her arms around his neck and pulled him to her. "You invigorate me, sir. May I have more, please?

❄

The windows of the church hall, their sills adorned with flickering candles, glowed like jewels on this Christmas Eve. An enormous, decorated pine tree stood to the left of the stage, and holly garlands bound in red satin ribbons festooned the walls. Towns-folk dressed in holiday finery packed the rows of folding chairs set up before the stage. Annabelle sat near the front between Rudy and Vince, and Charlie and Lance were seated on their right. Les Lowther and the Reverend and Mrs. Peterson sat on the end of the first row of chairs. The large contemporary hall was abuzz with chattering, but it instantly quieted when Chester Parker strode up the side steps to center stage. "Good evening, ladies and gentle-men, and welcome to the Crystal Falls annual Christmas pageant."

The crowd cheered and applauded, and Chester raised his palms to silence them. "Thank you," he said, once the applause died down. "I've been asked to say a few words, and I promise I'll keep it brief."

"Good," someone cried, eliciting chuckles from the assembly.

"Duly noted," Chester said. "As you know, Mrs. Maggie Jenkins has directed this pageant over the last many years. Unfor-tunately, that dear woman's health is failing. Please, keep her in your prayers." Then he leaned forward and affected a grave demeanor. "Now, I don't think it's a stretch to say that we were in a pickle, not knowing how we were going to pull off the pageant without Maggie. As many of you are aware, we were at our wits' end and seriously considered canceling altogether."

The audience stirred.

"No," a voice hollered.

"It just wouldn't be right," another added.

"But disaster was averted, my friends, when an angel appeared among us. You heard me. An angel!" Chester paused for dramatic effect before continuing. "That angel was in the form of one Ms. Olivia Barone."

Olivia was watching from the wings, and Chester motioned for her to join him on stage. She grimaced and waved a hand dismis-sively, but Chester persisted.

"Come on out here, Olivia."

There was no other option, but do as he asked, and Olivia

hiked across the stage to stand beside the sheriff. Chester draped an arm over Olivia's shoulder. "This wonderful young woman graciously agreed to step in and direct the pageant, and I hear she has a jingle-jangle, jim-dandy program lined up for us tonight." Chester gave Olivia's shoulder a paternal squeeze before releasing her. He clapped his hands as he crossed the stage, and the audience followed suit. Then he scooted down the steps to join his wife and friends in the audience.

"Thank you so much, and now let me thank *you*." Olivia spread her arms wide, acknowledging the crowd. "This has been a concerted effort. So many of you have contributed generously of your time and talents to make tonight's program possible. Of course, I'm sure you all know Rhett Dunbar, radio personality and songster extraordinaire." Olivia extended an open palm toward the wings, and Rhett bounded to center stage. He was a natural ham, and the audience applauded enthusiastically.

"Rhett has written some wonderful new material, which he is going to debut for you this evening." Olivia put her hands together, and once again, the audience joined in.

"I also want to thank Anne Ellis." Olivia motioned toward the keyboardist seated at the organ, and the graying matron waved a hand in the air.

"And now we begin." Olivia cried.

There was a groundswell of applause from the audience as the house lights dimmed. Then, after a brief flurry of activity as the actors found their places, the left side stage lights came up to reveal Timmy Corker. Wearing a red velvet parka and pants trimmed in white fur, with a matching hat, red gloves, tall black boots, a wide black belt, with a curling white wig on his head, and a long, white beard at his chin, Tim was a dead-ringer for Santa. He sat in a wing chair with Aiden McGill on his knee, and facing him were half a dozen small children, all dressed in their Christmas reds and greens. They sat cross-legged on the floorboards, forming a semi-circle before him.

Below and in front of the stage, Anne Ellis played the intro to Rhett's original *JINGLE-JOLLY SANTA*. They all sang:

"I saw Santa at the mall last night.
He took me on his knee.
My brother said he was a fake,
But he looked real to me.

"His Santa suit was soft and red,
His belt and boots were black,
He had candy-canes and presents,
In a great big Christmas sack.

"He was short and fat, and jolly,
And his beard was long and white,
And I thought, Oh, gee by golly,
It's Santa Claus, alright!

"Oh, jingle-jolly, old St. Nick,
You're real as you can be.
I saw you at the mall last night,
Beside the Christmas tree.

"Now, I believe with all my heart,
In you, dear Santa Claus.
So, promise you'll be good to me,
When you fly to my house.

"I'll leave you cookies and some milk,
And reindeer sugar, too.
So, jingle-jolly, old St. Nick,
Come down my chimney flue.

"I saw you at the mall last night,
Beside the Christmas tree.
Oh, jingle-jolly, old St. Nick,
You're real as you can be.

"Jingle-jolly! Oh, by golly!
Jingle-jolly, Santa Claus!"

The lights dimmed on the left side of the stage, and the main stage curtain opened to reveal a painted scrim depicting a country Christmas scene: bungalows dotting a snow-covered country lane that wove around a frozen pond and rime-frosted trees. Downstage perched on stools, were Rhett and Olivia. They had guitars in hand, and little children, dressed in festive holiday clothing sat at their feet. The two strummed the opening chords to Rhett's original *CHRISTMAS IN THE COUNTRY* composition.

They all sang:

> "Christmas in the city,
> Is spectacular, it's true.
> The city lights, the city sights,
> And city things to do.

> "The city windows beckon,
> Like magic, they appear.
> And Santaland's in Macy's,
> And he'll be there every year.

A couple of the older boys were dressed in jackets and caps, and one of them had a fake ax in hand. They entered and immediately searched for their Christmas tree.

> "But Christmas in the country,
> Has a charm that's all its own.
> Traditions that we cherish,
> The joys of hearth, and home."

Sleighbells chimed:

> *Ching, ching, ching, ching,*
> *Ching, ching, ching, ching.*

The boys grinned, gesturing at the real Christmas tree set off stage left.

"Christmas in the country,
It's where I want to be.
We'll dress up warm and head outside,
To find the perfect tree."

Then the boys crossed downstage to join the singers, and a girl entered. She was followed by a boy wearing a coat and knit cap. He carried a small jug of maple syrup wrapped with a red and green bow. The boy stood before the girl and mimed knocking on a door. She pretended to open it, and the boy thrust the gift toward her. They posed for a moment in a sweet tableau as the girl accepted the gift. Then they crossed down to join the others, all singing:

"Christmas in the country,
Though the pace is rather slow,
We send out Christmas greetings,
To everyone we know.

The country kitchen's fragrant,
With figs, and dates, and spice,
Christmas cookies baking,
And gingerbread to ice."

Two little children, dressed as elves, shook sleighbells, infusing the melody with a cheery, percussive sparkle.
Ching, ching, ching, ching,
Ching, ching, ching, ching.

"Christmas in the country,
It's where I want to be.
Where sleigh bells chime,
At Christmas time,
That's the place for me."

The lights dimmed on the main stage and came up on stage

left. There, Timmy Corker, still dressed in his Santa suit, was surrounded by several children, a few dressed as elves.

"And families are gathering,
For that special day,
Ms. Nick wrapped the presents,
And Santa's packed his sleigh."

The light stayed on the left and came back up on center stage.

"The pond is frozen solid,
The skaters glide and sway.
And sleds are flyin' down the hill,
Careening out' harm's way.
Sleighbells chime:
*Ching, ching, ching, ching,
Ching, ching, ching, ching.*

Olivia slipped into the wings while all the other children gathered around Rhett and continued the song:

"Christmas in the country,
Has a charm that's hard to beat.
Candles in the windows,
Garlands in the streets.

Yes, Christmas in the city,
Has a charm that's all its own.
But Christmas in the country,
Is home sweet, home sweet, home."

Backstage, Olivia stood behind the closed curtain. When the applause following the last number died down, she slipped in front of it, entering from the left. At the same time, Celia, Stacy Lowther, and Lizzy Corker entered as a group from stage right. All four of them were costumed as painted dolls, and they met downstage center. With faces made up in heavily applied pancake makeup, they wore stiff crinoline skirts and curly wigs atop their heads. Even before they opened their mouths, titters and laughter were heard from the audience.

Rhett hiked up the steps to the left wing and positioned himself just downstage of the women. His eyes met Olivia's and she gave a slight nod of her head. Then his callused fingertips strummed the strings of his outsized guitar, playing the opening bars to his original BAD GIRL SANTA. Anne joined in, fleshing out the accompaniment on the organ.

Stacie Lowther began the first lyric, leaning forward with her hands on her knees.

> "Dear Santa, I am writing you,
> This Christmas list of mine.
> Can't say I've been good this year,
> For that would be a lie.
>
> Dear Santa, I must now confess,
> The elves will tell you so.
> I haven't done just as I should.
> I guess you have to know…"

With hands clasped behind her back, Lizzy Corker shuffled forward, contritely, while warbling her lines:

> "I've been a bad girl, Santa,
> 'Cause good girls have no fun.
> Coal fills good girl's stockings,
> For the good things they have done.
>
> Bad girls may be naughty,
> But they score more than coal.
> Diamond rings, and pretty things,
> A mink-trimmed sable stole."

Celia muscled her way past the other two, her fists pressed saucily against her hips as she picked up the tune.

"Put 'em on your list, dear Santa,
Bring me what I ask.
I've been *bad* this year,
And then some,
You can bring me cash.

"I've been a bad girl, Santa,
'Cause good girls have no fun.
Coal fills up their stockings,
For the good things they have done."

Coming in like gangbusters, Olivia counted on her fingers while listing her transgressions in her soaring soprano:

"I cheated on my boyfriend, Santa,
I danced each night till dawn.
I drank too much hard liquor,
And passed out on the lawn.
I carried on with Conrad,
I canoodled some with Fred.
Darling Bradley loved me madly,
And I messed with his head.
Shameless as a floozie,
I lied, and fussed, and swore,
I carried on in Crystal town…"

At that line the audience roared its approval, and she had to pause until the din died down before continuing.

"And then I danced some more."

All three sang the chorus, gently rocking so their skirts swung like bells:

"Santa, I'm a bad girl,
All the boys, they say I'm hot.
They'll tell you that I'm awfully good,

But the truth is, I am not.

"Santa, jingling jolly bells,
Are festive as can be.
So, hang 'em on some muscled hunks,
Beneath my Christmas tree.

"Santa Claus, I'm writing you,
This fact, although it's sad.
I've been a bad girl all year long,
Dear Santa.
I've been bad, bad,
Bad, bad, BAD."

Olivia, Celia, Stacey Lowther, and Lizzy Corker bowed and curtsied to thunderous applause. Reverend Peterson and his wife appeared suitably shocked, but Charlie put two fingers to his lips and whistled shrilly.

Rising to his feet, he waved his arms about, hollering, "That's my girl," and encouraging the others to join him in a standing ovation.

Then the women scurried off behind the curtain. Moments later, the red velvet panels parted to reveal a stage now set as the traditional nativity scene. The lights came up on Aiden McGill, who had taken his place up-center. Downstage was the creche, flanked by Amelie, dressed as the Virgin Mary, and the boy portraying Joseph. All the other children, the angels and sheep, shepherds, stars, animals, and magi, were gathered around them.

Anne played the opening bars of LONG TIME AGO IN BETH-LEHEM on the organ, and Rhett strummed out the melody on guitar.

They all sang:

"Long time ago in Bethlehem,
So the Holy Bible say…"

As the children and Rhett sang, Olivia, Celia, Lizzie and

Stacey were making a hasty change; they removed their wigs, brushed their hair, and toned down their makeup. Then they shed their racy costumes and slipped into demure holiday outfits, Olivia's: a silky, red plaid skirt and a sequined sweater.

By the time the song had ended, the four floozies had transformed and were exiting down the stairs of the left wing to join the others for the final scene.

At the conclusion of the song, Aiden, having memorized his lines, spoke in a high clear voice that carried:

"And an angel of the Lord came upon them. Fear not, he said, for I bring you tidings of great joy."

The audience was rapt. More than one adult wept openly. This was the core of Christmas; the story of a child born into poverty who would bring his teachings of love and compassion into the world and forever change it.

"So, they hurried off and found Mary and Joseph, and the baby, who was lying in the manger," Aiden continued. "When they had seen him, they spread the word concerning what had been told them."

The spotlight found Amelie's innocent face. She looked out blindly at the darkened hall, hesitating while searching for her mother.

From the wings, where the four women and Timmy had gathered, Olivia whispered, "Go on, Amelie. Deliver your lines."

Amelie trembled, and seeing her distress, Aiden smiled at her encouragingly. She returned his smile with a tremulous one of her own and then faced the audience.

"But Mary trea-sured up all those things and pondered them in her heart."

At the sound of Amelie's liquid silver voice, so much voice for so small a girl, there was an audible gasp from those assembled, and everyone present hung on this precious child's words.

"The shep-herds returned," Amelie recited.

"Glorifying God for all the things they had heard and seen," Aiden said. "Which was just as they had been told."

At his final line, Anne Ellis played the opening chords to Rhett's original CHILD OF ANGELS.

Amelie's voice wafted sweetly throughout the hall:

> "On a cold, dark winter's night,
> Rose a star in the sky so bright.
> It shone all around on a little town,
> And a manger bare and slight.
>
> "There in that manger, bare and slight,
> Was born Child of angels, most Holy Light."

Anne took over, pulling out all the stops and playing a rousing chorus, while the entire cast assembled on stage.

All the other children, those dressed as elves or in street clothes, entered carrying battery-operated candles. They split, half to stand downstage right and the other half, downstage left. At the same time, Rhett, with his guitar in hand, bounded up the side steps and came to stand stage left of the nativity scene, and Timmy, still dressed in his Santa suit, joined by Olivia, Celia, Lizzie, and Stacey crossed to the right.

The entire cast sang:

> "Child of angels,
> Oh, Holy Light,
> Come to save us,
> From sin and plight.
>
> Bread of heaven,
> Food for the soul,
> You heal the broken,
> And make them whole.
> Child of angels,
> Pure Love Divine,
> Sweet Redeemer,

Of mankind."

At the bridge, the other voices dropped out. Unaccompanied, Amelie's dulcet soprano wafted throughout the hall.

"There in that manger bare and slight,
Was born a child of Angels, most Holy Light."

The rest of the cast joined in, singing in four-part harmony as the organ swelled. They brought the songfest to its satisfying conclusion with the ancient Christmas carol, *ADESTE FIDELES, and Timmy waved his arms about encouraging the audience to sing along:*

"Venite Adoremus,Venite Adoremus,Venite
Adoremus,Dominum."

Then the house lights as well as all the stage lights came up, and they finished with a reprise of *LONG TIME AGO IN BETHLE-HEM,* the lyrics of which had been printed on the programs:

"Hush now, hear the angels sing,
New king born today.
For man shall live forever more,
Because of Chri-ist-mas day.

Because of Chri-ist-mas day.
Because of Chri-ist-mas DAY."

Despite the late hour on this holiest of nights, the streets and sidewalks of Crystal Falls town center were aglow with fairy lights and bustling with activity. It was ten-thirty, an hour when, under normal circumstances, the central thoroughfare would have been deserted. But tonight, Main Street was clogged with a scattering of adults and throngs of youngsters. Several parents circulated, passing out cookies and little paper cups of hot chocolate. But for the most part, the little ones entertained themselves. They whooped and hollered, threw snowballs at one another, and streaked around in joyful abandon, shedding all the tension of their pent-up jitters and celebrating their stellar performances.

Amelie and her mother, Gabriella, stood on the sidewalk, taking it all in.

"Great job, Amelie," Aiden McGill burst upon them, a gap-toothed smile splitting his freckled face. "Hello, Mrs. García." He thrust out his hand. "Aiden McGill!"

"Si, Mister Narrator," Gabriella said, shaking the boy's hand. "Good job, yourself!"

"May Amelie come with me for a little while?" Aiden gestured toward a group of fellow junior thespians. "We're having a game of tag."

Gabriella looked at her daughter, and Amelie met her mother's gaze and shrugged.

"Si! You go play." Gabriella shooed Amelie away. "Mama will go inside. You stay close by, Amelie."

Nesbitt's was packed. It appeared as though the entire audience, except for Reverend Carroll and his wife, and a few adults who were supervising the children outside, had gravitated to the public house for a post-show toddy. Charlie was behind the bar and in his Zen, slinging drinks double-time, and Celia had pitched in to help. The two of them had fallen into an easy rhythm and seemed to work well in tandem.

Olivia sat at the end of the bar, a place of honor normally reserved for the town's gossips and unofficial newsmongers. She and Rhett, who stood on her left, were basking in their glory, accepting congratulations from one and all on their brilliantly successful pageant. Lance was seated on her right sharing in their triumph. Someone had draped Timmy's Santa jacket over Olivia's shoulders, and she wore it regally as though it were a queen's ermine robe. Rhett's Santa hat still sat jauntily atop his head, and he'd slipped on Timmy's beard. But now he wore the beard beneath his chin, rather than on his face, which allowed him to quaff the draft Charlie had set before him. So, his appearance was droll, to say the least.

Two hours later, the children had been gathered up by their parents and family members to be taken home and put snugly in their beds. And most of the other adults had toddled along themselves. Only a few diehards remained.

Charlie poured himself a Scotch and then refilled Lance's glass. Then he came from around the bar and put two fingers in his mouth. When his shrill whistle cut the air, all eyes turned to him. Having everyone's attention, he raised his glass. "Tonight, I am the happiest man on the planet. After all these years of being a loner, I find I have a family. So, here's to my lovely daughter, Olivia." He turned to her, holding his glass aloft. "Welcome home, darlin'!"

"Here, here," the patrons raised their glasses and toasted.

"To Olivia and Charlie," they cried.

Then Charlie plunked down on the stool next to Olivia's. Raising his glass once more, he looked at her. "Daughter, you've quite outdone yourself."

"I had it easy." Olivia touched his glass with hers. Then she turned to Rhett. "The big guy did all the heavy lifting."

Rhett slapped his palms to his chest and shook his head. "Babe, you were the driving force. Heck, you made me *work*. And I loved it. I owe you big time. I have a new Christmas album, thanks to your badgering."

"He's right," Lance said, putting an arm around Olivia and planting a tiny kiss on her forehead. "You are nothing short of *amazing*."

"Olivia, Livy lay ah!" Olivia sang tipsily.

They all laughed. Although they were weary, their faces wore smiles of contentment.

"Dad?" Olivia looked up at Charlie.

"Oh, that Dad part. It's music to my ears," Charlie said.

Olivia grinned. "About the sign out front…"

"What of it?"

"You know: Nesbitt's…the hand? What's with that?"

"Oh-ho! The hand." Charlie chuckled. "You may be a blue blood by marriage, my dear, but you're a Nesbitt by birth. And do you have any idea what that means?"

Intrigued, Olivia leaned in. "Absolutely no idea where this is going."

"Nice bit. That's what it means," Charlie said. "You'll be happy to know that you and I are descended from a long line of colorful villains and rogues. As it was told to me by your great grand-mama, our esteemed ancestor was fleeing from the law. Back in the old country, mind you. As the story goes, he'd been gravely wounded in a sword fight. While attempting to fend off his would-be captors, his hand was nearly severed at the wrist. Barely eluding his foes, he somehow managed to jump aboard a ship bound for America. No sooner had he done so than he slashed through the bit of sinew, all that connected the poor appendage to his wrist, and tossed the useless hand onto the dock. 'Take that,' he taunted as the ship set sail, leaving his angry pursuers on the wharf below. 'It's a nice bit for you.'"

"So, you're saying…"

"I'm saying it's probably a crock of malarkey, but I'm willing to bet you come by your dramatic streak quite honestly, my dear."

"'Nice bit?'" Olivia arched a brow. "Not really buying it, Dad."

Lance's sapphire eyes sparkled with admiration as he gazed at her. "Oh, yeah. A nice bit, indeed."

FIFTEEN
COUNTRY CHRISTMAS

On this, one of the longest nights of the year, a good many Crystal Falls residents had left their Christmas lights on. They twinkled from rooftops and lamp posts and window frames. Perhaps this display was meant as a beacon to help guide Santa on his way, or maybe it was simply a show of holiday spirit. But during that long, long night, if St. Nick and his reindeer had, indeed, sailed over the rooftops, they'd have surely made many stops in this little town that knew how to celebrate this happiest of seasons in a big way.

In the wee hours, before dawn embroidered the horizon with golden threads, children awakened from their slumbers, vivid dreams of hoped-for gifts still fresh in their minds. Siblings whispered excitedly to one another, debating whether it was too early to rouse their sleeping parents and tear into their Christmas bounty, while the more intrepid little souls crept from their beds to open stocking gifts before the rest of the household had arisen.

The day staff of the Samaritan homeless center had clocked in early so that they might spend time, later in the afternoon, with their own families. In the large, stainless-steel kitchen, cooks were busy preparing special meals to bring cheer to those who had no family of their own.

Mercy Hospital's nursing staff and physicians, God's own angels on Earth, had risen even earlier than usual to care for their patients, those who were diseased, injured, or dying. But in the maternity ward, a healthy Christmas baby was being delivered, a new life and a promise for the future.

By noon, Les and Stacy Lowther were presiding over their large clan in their tastefully decorated home. They'd assembled in the living room where garlands of holly hung in swags from the mantle top, and a giant Christmas tree, strung with lights and adorned with ornaments, dominated one corner. Dressed in their holiday attire, the adult children and their partners had taken every available seat, and the grandkids sat cross-legged on the floor, eagerly waiting for the fun to begin.

"All right," Stacy said. "Is everybody ready?"

"Yes!" was the resounding answer.

"Go!" Les cried, and the children needed no more encouragement. They ripped into their wrapped gifts, sending ribbons and tissue paper flying.

Several blocks away, the elegant Federalist-style home of Timmy and Lizzy Corker sat astride two half-acre parcels. Large ceramic urns filled with poinsettias flanked the massive double doorway, which was framed with holly garlands, miniature strung lights, and red ribbons.

Inside, Lizzy glanced at the hall clock. It was after one o'clock. "Are you dressed?" she called up the stairs to her husband.

"Ugh," Timmy grunted, once again struggling into his Santa suit. "Getting there."

"Hurry up, dear. We need to be at the homeless shelter in half an hour." Lizzy made her way to the Christmas tree in the front room, humming to herself as she went. It was a towering live spruce, prominently displayed in a large bay window that looked out over an expansive lawn, now blanketed in snow. She gathered up wrapped gifts from beneath the tree and deposited them, one after another, into Timmy's red velvet Santa bag.

"Ho, ho, ho!" Timmy huffed as he tramped down the stairs, his round face beaming. "I've got something special for you, Mrs. Claus."

Lizzy turned to her husband, who was now a vision of the Jolly Old Elf himself. "Is that so?" she asked, a twinkle in her eye. "You of all people must know, Santa, I've been a bad girl."

"Oh, yes. And that is why you get a very good gift. Come here, and I'll show you."

Lizzy laughed merrily as she crossed the distance to Timmy. He'd planted himself on the first step and was enjoying the fact that, in that spot, he towered over her. From his pocket, he withdrew a tiny, beautifully wrapped package and then held it out before him.

The sun was already past its zenith when Chester Parker and his wife stood at the entryway to their sprawling ranch-style house. Broad smiles lit their faces as they welcomed their son and daughter-in-law.

"Merry Christmas," cried the young man, who was a younger, leaner version of his dad.

"Jeremy, Sarah! Hello, hello! Come in out of the cold." Mrs. Parker waved the couple in.

Once inside, Jeremy placed a tiny newborn, who had been swaddled in a blue blanket, in Chester's awaiting arms. Then, proudly and with great tenderness, Chester carried his new grandson into the living room. There, he began pointing out decorations on the Christmas tree.

"And see this one." He indicated a small brass ornament engraved with the image of an infant and the year 1990. "We bought that the year your daddy was born."

"Going to have to get a new one this year, Dad," Jeremy said.

At two o'clock, Celia seated herself in her cheery kitchen nook and snatched up her cell phone. "Merry Christmas," she cried.

"And to you, Mom."

That familiar voice, coming to her from over six thousand miles away, caused Celia's throat to constrict with sudden emotion. But she put a smile in her own voice. "How are you, Chelsea?" Celia cut her gaze to a framed photograph on the mantle. It was an image of a fresh-faced young woman clothed in standard-issue army fatigues. Her head was a mass of glossy, dark curls and she wore a determined grin on a heartbreakingly earnest face.

Celia's heart flip-flopped.

"Just fine, Mom. I've finally settled in."

"What's it like there, sweetie?"

"It's pretty cool. Base Bagram is like a miniature city. There's a recreational center with internet and video games, TVs, and a fitness center. And the food is good, lots of choices. Besides the cafeteria, we have a burger joint, a Dairy Queen, and even a pizza parlor. I'm okay. What's new in Crystal Falls?"

"Oh, you wouldn't believe it; I may have a new man in my life."

"No!" Chelsea exclaimed. "It's about time. Who's the lucky fellow?"

"I'll get back to you on that. First, let me see if this is going anywhere. The guy hasn't even asked me out on a date yet."

"Oh, my gosh!" Chelsea's tone conveyed delight. "Well, I hope it works out. You've been alone too long, Mom."

"Yeah. And I have a new gal pal, Olivia Barone, although I'm quite certain she's going to lose that last name and darned quick." Cee-Cee chattered away, filling Chelsea in on the latest news. Olivia's search for her father, the epic fight at Nesbitt's, the Christmas pageant, and all the recent comings and goings in Crystal Falls.

On the other side of the ocean, and a continent away, Chelsea plopped down on her bunk. There was an eight-hour time difference between them; her Christmas dinner had been hours ago. But Celia's gift to her daughter and the care package that had shipped from the Crystal Falls Antioch Primitive Baptist Church sat unopened on the bed beside her. She'd wanted to wait for this moment, when she felt, despite the distance that separated them, that she was in the presence of her mother and surrounded by her love.

"Hey, Mom, I'm going to open my gifts now." Her eyes fell upon the red votive candle she'd placed atop her nightstand. It was her small way of commemorating Christmas in Afghanistan. "And that's great news," she laughed, as she cut through the packing tape on one of the boxes. "I can't wait to meet your new friend. But about this mysterious man…you've *got* to give me some details."

Back in Crystal Falls, five blocks from the city center, in a humble one-story dwelling, the García family celebrated their first Christmas in the community. Furnished with donated cast-offs and thrift shop bargains, the modest house the church had provided was spotlessly clean, and they thought it was heaven. Here, they found themselves surrounded by a host of compassionate church friends and welcoming neighbors. Best of all, there were no gangs. Miraculously given a chance at a new life, one with a future, they counted their blessings.

Gabriella, Amelie, and her older brother, Luis, were gathered around the kitchen table, preparing a traditional Guatemalan Christmas feast. Mrs. García chopped tomatillos and onions for a piquant salsa verde. At the same time, Amelie was giving her older brother instructions, explaining how to prepare the festive red and black tamales, chicken colorados wrapped in banana leaves and sweet rice tamales negros with mole.

"¿Te gusta?" *Like this?* The slightly built teen rolled shredded chicken in a banana leaf.

"Mas ordenado, Luis." *More neatly, Luis.* Amelie reached over and tucked in the filling of his disreputable-looking tamale. Then she placed the bundle in a greased baking dish.

"Ah!" Disgusted, the boy threw his hands in the air. "Esto es trabajo para las mujeres." *This is women's work.*

"Manuel," Gabriella called. "Ven, mira el pavo." *The turkey.*

In the next moment, her husband sprinted into the tiny kitchen. In his arms was a delicate-looking lamb figure with a red ribbon encircling its neck. This whimsical form was comprised of nothing more than Spanish moss and pine branches, but Amelie clapped her hands in delight at the sight of it.

"Si, Mama." Manuel said. "Pero primero, el cordero de Navideño." *But first, the Christmas lamb.*

"Oh, Papá, que hermosa!" *How beautiful,* Amelie exclaimed.

Mr. García placed the lamb on a chair and then turned to his son. He affected a stern expression. "Luis, en los estados unidos, eso del trabajo de mujer, no existe." *There is no women's work in the United States.* Manuel smiled indulgently at his son and ruffled the boy's hair. "Real men cook."

Gabriella and Amelie laughed.

Manuel crossed to behind his wife and wrapped his sinewy arms around her waist. She angled her head toward him, and he kissed her cheek. But in the next moment, Gabriella feigned annoyance and squirmed out of his grasp. "Manuel, el pavo!"

Amelie and Luis patted their father's back and steered him in the direction of the oven and the turkey roasting within. "Los hombres tambien saben concinar, Papá." *Real men cook!*

❄

Mercy Hospital was a modern, five-story, steel-and-glass structure. There, in a single room on the second floor, a slip of a woman lay sleeping in a narrow bed and fenced in by side rails. She was thin and frail-looking, cheekbones prominent, her skin nearly translucent. Yet, she possessed an ethereal beauty.

Awakening with a start, she stared blindly at the ceiling from where celestial voices called to her. Then her gaze fell upon the windowsill where potted plants crowded next to one another, vainly seeking a bashful sun. From there, her eyes drifted to the scene beyond. Outside, the mid-winter light was pale, the sky milky. It had stopped snowing, and on the horizon, the hem of night was falling. A single bright star winked on high.

She turned toward a bedside table awash in Christmas cards from her many friends, colleagues, and students. Among them was an oversized card signed by all the participants in this year's Christmas pageant. *Merry Christmas, Maggie, Get Well Soon, Maggie.*

The corners of her mouth curled up in a small smile.

More good wishes, greeting cards and photographs, papered the opposite wall of the small room.

"A life well-lived," Maggie murmured as she began to let slip her moorings to this world. "A life well loved."

Suddenly, the star was in her room! It pulsed with an otherworldly radiance, casting an aura about the cramped space.

Maggie's smile grew wider, her expression transfixed. "I'm coming," she whispered. And for the last time on this Earth, she closed her eyes.

Two hundred miles to the south, Eric lounged in front of his enormous flatscreen TV, vainly trying to conjure some Christmas spirit. He sipped his ridiculously expensive Courvoisier from an oversized brandy snifter and gazed out his picture window at the panoramic view of the city lights.

But it wasn't working.

He glanced around at his recently redecorated interior. The

designer had chosen a neutral color palette, pale gray walls, darker gray upholstery, and taupe-colored linen drapery. The monochromatic scheme was relieved by accents in crimson and gold, a few fringed pillows, and a large hand-thrown ceramic bowl. The gleaming chrome and glass occasional tables and sleek, low-slung sofas were attractive but cold-looking with their metal-framed arms and legs. A silver foil tree placed in front of the picture window did little to warm the place. And yet, the contemporary décor suited him, and he felt right at home.

Still, something was missing.

At the commercial break, Eric's eyes wandered to a framed photograph displayed on a side table. It was of Olivia in happier times, her dazzling smile so infectious. And the sight of it caused his heart to contract. He remembered the day he'd taken it. It had been shortly after they'd married. When they been so deliriously infatuated with one another, and life had stretched before them with bright promise.

"What happened?" Eric muttered. But, although he refused to acknowledge it, he knew the answer.

"Here's to you, doll." Eric raised his glass and toasted her image. "Merry Christmas. Happy New Year. Happy life."

It was a dark, bitterly cold evening, and the commercial outskirts of Crystal Falls looked like a barren, no-man's-land. A gusty wind drove clouds of fine snow pellets between empty buildings and across deserted parking lots while shredding pale moonlight overhead.

There was not a sign of life anywhere.

But Rhett hardly noticed. He was eager to return to his radio studio, a tiny windowless room housing one comfortable desk chair and a massive soundboard with a swivel stool set before it. When he closed the insulated door to his inner sanctum, the solitude that enveloped him was like an old companion. This was home for him, a couple of mics, his guitar, and thousands of faceless listeners who were his friends. He crammed a plush red Santa hat on his head and ponied up to a mic.

Rhett was in his element, a lonely man spinning Christmas cheer, sending his original tunes out across the airwaves. He had no expectations. All he hoped was that a song or two might strike a chord and give pleasure to someone out there. He was the song man, and this was the best he could do.

"Howdy, folks! Rhett Dunbar here, bringing it to you at 1370 on your AM dial. It was another gorgeous day out there, and now that all the gifts have been opened, old Tom Turkey picked to his bones, I hope you'll spend some time with me this Christmas evening…"

Olivia was streaming 1370 AM radio from her iPad as she sat before her dressing table, fastening a strand of pearls around her neck. She smiled at the sound of Rhett's voice coming to her from over the airwaves to her device. After adjusting the necklace, she turned her head from side to side, eyeing her reflection in the mirror. She'd piled her chestnut-colored locks atop her head to show off her best pearl drop earrings. And since Annabelle had decided they were to dine late, she'd applied a bit more eye makeup than usual and eschewed her standard pink lip-gloss for a true red lipstick. The form-fitting, black velvet, strapless sheath she'd donned clung to her curves like Saran Wrap. But Annabelle had insisted she wear it, cautioning her that, "You've got it. So, you might as well flaunt it, dear. Believe me, *it* won't last forever!"

Olivia pivoted to Milo, who was intently watching her from his vantage point atop the bed. "What say you, old man? Is it too much?"

Just then the doorbell pealed, and Milo sprang to his feet yapping excitedly.

In the next moment, Annabelle called up the stairs. "Olivia, will you get that? I'm up to my elbows in the kitchen."

"Sure thing," she hollered, powering down her laptop, and coming to her feet. Then she crossed to Milo and scooped him up in her arms, and the little sentry immediately quieted. Her gray-green eyes met his endless brown ones, and Olivia's heart melted. With a red and green plaid bow tied about his neck, he was a very dashing doggie companion.

"It's Christmas, my love. Let's get to it!"

SIXTEEN
THE CHARM

N ESBITT'S severed hand was a flickering beacon in the lightly falling snow that was blanketing Crystal Falls, but the tavern was dark, with a closed sign on its door. The little tabletop Christmas tree gleamed cheerily in Charlie's apartment over the pub, and Alley Cat lay curled in his chair, but the proprietor was nowhere to be seen.

Meanwhile, the dining room table at Mrs. Bow's Charming Manner was set with Annabelle's best china. Antique cut-glass goblets and newly polished silverware sparkled in the refracted light shed by the myriad crystals of the Waterford chandelier overhead. Vince and Charlie sat on one side of the table, Lance and Olivia on the other. Annabelle occupied the hostess chair nearest the kitchen, and Rudy was seated in the host chair opposite her. They were all laughing and chatting, passing dishes, and helping to serve one another.

"You must try this," Annabelle said, holding a casserole before Charlie.

"What is it?" Charlie asked.

Annabelle laughed. "Humble pie."

"Oh, I've had quite enough of that," he said, grinning.

"No, really. It's my world-famous spinach and parmesan savory pie."

Charlie held out his plate. "In that case, I'll take two helpings."

"Olivia, I hear you've been offered a job," Rudy said.

"Yes. After the pageant, a gentleman approached me. It seems there's an opening at the community college in Millbrook. They're looking for someone to teach music and direct the choir."

"What a coincidence." Annabelle arched a brow, casting a side-long glance at Olivia, who snickered at the inside joke.

"I'd say that was right up your alley, sweetheart." Charlie's eyes gleamed with a father's pride.

"Well, that didn't take long." Vince caught Olivia's gaze. "You've made quite a mark for yourself here, Livy."

"That she has," Lance said, smiling broadly at Olivia. "I believe Camelot's true queen miraculously appeared in our hayfield just in the nick of time."

"Yes, Annabelle agreed. "Just in the Jolly Old Saint Nick of time!"

Milo lay curled under the table, his head resting on Olivia's foot. When Lance's hand sneaked beneath the tabletop, his ears perked up, and his eyes followed the hand as it searched for Olivia's.

Merlin was sprawled out across from Milo. Unimpressed, the Lab yawned, and putting his shaggy head in his paws, closed his eyes.

On the flip side of the table, Lance and Olivia glanced at the happy faces of those gathered around them. Then they searched each other's eyes and smiled.

Beneath the table, Lance's hand finally connected with Olivia's and the two threaded fingers. At that, Merlin's head shot up, and Milo rose to all fours. The Yorkie trotted to Merlin and reposi-tioned himself before his new man bud.

From that moment on, those two would be like peas in a pod, one very big pea and one tiny pee-pee.

"Woof," Merlin rumbled softly. Then he hunkered back down and protectively positioned a meaty paw before his wee companion.

"Grr," Milo breathed before closing his eyes.

And as canine dreams flooded his consciousness, and he gave himself over to snuffled snores, it was the foreign word *Camelot* that resonated in Milo's brain.

He didn't know what it meant. He only knew that it was good.

THE END

INDEX OF SONGS

ANNABELLE & FRIENDS' HOLIDAY RECIPES

OLIVIA BARONE'S BUTTERNUT SQUASH SOUP

Serves 6 – 8

INGREDIENTS

1 butternut squash
3 TBS extra virgin olive oil
3 TBS butter
½ cup chopped onion
1 clove garlic, minced
1 tsp salt
1 tsp good quality yellow curry powder
1/8 tsp cayenne pepper
1 cup organic chicken broth
1 cup half and half or cream
¼ cup 100 % maple syrup

PREPARATION

- Preheat oven to 350-degrees F.
- Wash squash and prick skin to allow steam to escape. Microwave on high for 5 minutes (or until squash can be easily cut in half lengthwise.)
- Bake in an oiled casserole or baking pan in a 350-degree oven for 50 minutes to 1¼ hours, until squash is very

tender. When cool enough to handle, scoop out squash into a medium sized bowl, and discard skin.

- Melt butter in a large saucepan and sauté onion until it is translucent (about 5 minutes).
- Add squash, salt, curry powder and cayenne pepper and continue cooking for about 1 minute.
- Add chicken broth and maple syrup, and simmer until squash is beginning to break down (about 10 minutes).
- Puree in a blender or food processor in two to three batches, never letting squash mixture fill more than 2/3 of the blender or processor.
- Transfer to a large saucepan and add half and half or cream. Stir until well-blended and heat till simmering.
- Sample a spoonful and adjust cayenne pepper and maple syrup to taste.

To serve:

Serve in large mugs or wide shallow soup bowls with crusty French bread as an accompaniment.

Note: The heat of the cayenne pepper combined with the earthy squash and sweet maple syrup deliver a satisfying umami that warms the heart on crisp Autumn days.

ANNABELLE'S HUNGARIAN GOULASH

Yields about 8 hearty servings

INGREDIENTS

3 ½ - 4 pounds beef chuck roast, cut into 2-inch cubes
salt & pepper to taste
2 TBS of vegetable oil
2 onions, coarsely chopped
2 TBS of olive oil
½ tsp of salt
2 TBS of Hungarian paprika (sweet smoked paprika works too)
2 tsp of caraway seeds
1 tsp black pepper
1 tsp of dried marjoram
½ tsp of ground thyme
½ tsp cayenne pepper
4 cups of chicken broth
½ cup of tomato paste
5 cloves of garlic, crushed
2 TBS of balsamic vinegar
1 tsp of white sugar
½ tsp of salt, or to taste
1 bay leaf

PREPARATION

- Season the beef with salt and pepper.
- Heat the vegetable oil in a large skillet on high heat.
- Cook the beef until well-browned, about 5 minutes. (In batches so beef is not crowded.)
- Using a slotted spoon, transfer the beef to a large, heavy pot or Dutch oven.
- Leave the drippings in the skillet.
- Lower the skillet heat to medium and add the onions.
- Drizzle olive oil over the onions and season with ½ tsp of salt.
- Cook until the onions are softened, about 5 minutes.
- Add the onions to the pot with the beef.
- In the skillet, stir in the paprika, caraway seeds, pepper, marjoram, thyme, and cayenne pepper and cook until fragrant, about 1-minute.
- Add 1 cup of chicken broth to the spices, stir.
- Transfer the mixture to the pot with the beef and onions.
- Add 3 cups of chicken broth to the pot and stir.
- Add the tomato paste, garlic, vinegar, sugar, ½ tsp of salt, and the bay leaf to the pot, and mix until all ingredients are well-incorporated.
- Turn the heat to high and bring to a boil.
- Reduce the heat to low and simmer uncovered for 2.25 to 2.5 hours, until the liquid is reduced, and the meat is fork tender.

To serve:

Serve over buttered pappardelle noodles or the pasta of your choice.

GABRIELLA GARCIA'S CHICKEN COLORADOS

Yields 6 servings

INGREDIENTS
SPICE MIXTURE
1 tsp Mexican oregano
½ tsp ground chili powder
½ tsp ancho chili powder
½ tsp turmeric
½ tsp cumin
½ tsp ground cinnamon
½ tsp coriander
½ tsp thyme
½ tsp epazote (if available)
¼ tsp allspice
¼ tsp ground cloves

SAUCE MIXTURE
1 tsp finely shredded orange peel
juice of 1 orange
½ tsp salt
½ tsp freshly ground peppercorn
1 cup chopped onion (1 large)

5 cloves of garlic, minced
1 – 14.5 oz can stewed tomatoes

CHICKEN
2-½ to 3 pounds chicken thighs with bone and or drumsticks

BANANA LEAVE WRAPS
12 banana leaves wiped clean with a damp paper towel

PICKLED ONIONS
1 red onion sliced and separated into rings
¼ cup white wine vinegar
¼ tsp salt
½ tsp dried oregano, crushed
¼ tsp freshly ground peppercorn
3 cloves garlic, minced.

PREPARATION

- Prepare the chicken, which may be done 24 hours before assembling the bundles:
- In a small bowl blend together the first 11 ingredients, then divide the spice mixture between two small bowls.
- Sprinkle one bowl of the spice mixture over the chicken and press it into the flesh. Roast in a covered casserole at 300-degree F for 45 minutes (or bake in a crock pot at low setting for 6 hours. When chicken is cool enough to handle, skin, debone, and cut or shred meat into pieces. Set aside or refrigerate if preparing the bundles the next day.

Prepare the pickled onions, which may be done ahead of time and refrigerated:

Place sliced onion into a stainless-steel pan and cover with boiling water. Let stand one minute and then drain well. Return onions to the pan and add vinegar, salt, oregano, peppercorn, and garlic. Bring to a boil and then reduce heat to low and cover.

Simmer for 5 minutes. Remove onions and brine to a small bowl and cool for about 45 minutes.

Prepare the banana leaves:

Cut the banana leaves into 12" X 9" rectangles, loosely roll up and place in a steamer basket over, but not touching, boiling water. Cover and steam for 20 – 30 minutes until pliable but still retaining their shape. Remove and cool.

Prepare the sauce:

In a blender, process stewed tomatoes, orange juice, onion, and garlic. Add the other half of the spice mixture and process until well-blended. Pour sauce into a large measuring cup or small bowl.

Assemble the bundles:

- Preheat oven to 375-degrees F
- Mound about ½ cup of shredded chicken on each banana leaf and flatten.
- Pour about 2 TBS sauce over chicken and wrap in the banana leaf, folding long sides over first and then folding the short sides to make a bundle. Bundles may be tied with kitchen twine or secured with toothpicks or small wooden skewers that have been soaked in water.
- Place bundles in a single layer in a lightly greased casserole and cover with lid.
- Bake at 375-degree F for 1 hour.

To serve:

Carefully remove banana leaves from cooked chicken and serve topped with pickled onions.

Recommended side dishes:

Black beans and steamed white rice or Mexican Rice (see following recipe).

Note: If banana leaves are unavailable, wrap bundles in foil to bake, or reheat chicken and serve with sauce and pickled onions in warmed corn or flour tortillas.

GABRIELLA GARCIA'S MEXICAN RICE

Yields about 3 cups (4 – 6 servings)

INGREDIENTS
2 TBS extra virgin olive oil
1 onion, finely chopped (about 1 cup)
2 garlic cloves, minced (about 1 tsp)
1- ¼ cups medium or long-grain white rice (I prefer Basmati.)
1- ½ cups chicken stock (substitute vegetable stock for vegetarian)
1- 10-oz can diced tomatoes and green chilies (I prefer Ro-Tel although diced fresh or cooked tomatoes may be substituted, but add an additional ¼ - 1 cup stock)
½ tsp salt
½ tsp coriander
½ tsp cumin
½ tsp turmeric

PREPARATION

- Sauté rice in olive oil for one minute.
- Add chopped onion and garlic and cook, stirring often, until about half the rice is lightly toasted (no more than three minutes).

- Add broth, diced tomatoes and all other ingredients.
- Simmer gently until all liquid is absorbed and rice is tender, about 20 minutes, stirring often and adding more broth if rice is too dry.

Note: This flavorful rice makes a delicious side to any Mexican entrée and is great reheated with a little more stock the next day.

ANNABELLE'S HUMBLE PIE

Yields 1 savory pie

INGREDIENTS
   1 bunch fresh spinach, trimmed and washed
   1/3 cup olive oil plus 1 tsp
   2 onions, chopped
   1 leek, cleaned well, white part only, finely chopped (discard green tops)
   12 sheets filo pastry
   ½ stick (4 TBS) butter
   1½ - 2 cups grated parmesan
   1 cup semi-dried tomatoes, chopped (see recipe below)
   2 eggs
   salt & fresh ground pepper

PREPARATION

- Preheat oven to 425-degrees F.
- Plunge spinach into a pot of boiling water, and boil until just wilted.
- Drain well, squeezing out excess moisture in paper towels, and chop finely.
- Heat 1/3 cup of oil in a large pan over medium heat.

- Cook onions and leek, stirring constantly for about 10 minutes or until golden then set aside to cool.
- Cut pastry sheets in half widthways so you have 24 sheets.
- Layer 12 sheets on top of each other, brushing each sheet with melted butter, and place in the base of a greased 9" X 12" baking pan.
- Combine spinach/onion mixture, ricotta, parmesan, tomatoes, and eggs in a large bowl. Season with salt and pepper and spread over the pastry base.
- Repeat process with remaining filo and butter, and place on top of ricotta mixture.
- Brush top with 1 tsp olive oil.
- Bake for 15 minutes at 425 degrees, then reduce heat to 350 degrees and bake for an additional 20 – 30 minutes or until pastry is golden.

Serve warm or at room temperature.

JANE GENNARELLI'S SEMI-DRIED TOMATOES

Yields about 2 cups

INGREDIENTS

1¼ lb small grape or cherry tomatoes, all about the same size
1/8 tsp fine salt (updated from 1/4 tsp)
¼ tsp each: dried thyme, dried basil, dried oregano (optional)
2 tsp olive oil for brushing
oil for covering (optional, see note)

PREPARATION

- Preheat oven to 300-degrees F.
- Cut tomatoes in half lengthwise. If using larger tomatoes, cut out the core.
- Arrange the halved tomatoes over a baking sheet lined with parchment paper, cut sides up. (Do not use an aluminum baking sheet as the acid in the tomato will react with the metal.) Brush (or spray) lightly with olive oil. Sprinkle with salt. Then, after one hour of baking sprinkle with the dried herbs.
- Bake for 2 hours at 300°F, and then check degree of dryness. You want them pliable like dried fruit, and not completely dried out. If you don't need them right away,

you may turn off the oven and let the tomatoes sit in the oven to dry in the residual heat for another half hour (depends on how dry they already are).

- Store in a jar or sealed container the fridge for up to a few days.

To serve:

Incorporate these semi-dried tomatoes in pasta dishes and salads for a piquant taste of summer.

Notes: Semi-dried tomatoes still retain some moisture, so unless submerged in oil, they will get moldy when stored longer. For longer storage, place them in a jar tightly packed and cover with olive or sunflower oil. Add a garlic clove and more dried herbs—basil, thyme, oregano—for added zip.

GABRIELLA GARCIA'S SALSA VERDE

Makes about 2 cups

INGREDIENTS
- 1½ lbs. (8 – 10) tomatillos
- 3 TBS olive oil
- ½ cup coarsely chopped white onion
- 2 garlic cloves, minced
- ½ cup cilantro leaves
- 1 TBS fresh lime juice
- 2 jalapeño peppers or 2 serrano peppers, stemmed, seeded, and chopped
- Salt to taste

PREPARATION

- Preheat oven to 350 degrees F.
- Line baking dish with aluminum foil.
- Cut tomatillos into halves (or quarters, if very large).
- Pour olive oil in foil-lined pan, and add tomatillos, cut side down.
- Sprinkle chopped onion around tomatillos.

- Roast for 10 – 15 minutes until starting to soften, then remove from oven and flip tomatillos to cut side up, and roast for another 10 minutes.
- Process all ingredients in a food processor.

To serve:

Serve cold or at room temperature as a dip with tortilla chips. Also wonderful slathered over chicken thighs and baked on a sheet pan with your choice of vegetables.

ANNE ALEXANDER'S BUFFET SALMON

Makes about 12 servings

INGREDIENTS

1 - 2½ lb. salmon fillet (Purchase the largest filet that will fit nicely on whatever serving dish you plan on using for your buffet with enough room on the perimeter for a garnish of lemon wedges.)

1 tsp olive oil

salt and pepper

¼ - ½ cup mayonnaise (depending on the size of your fillet)

¼ cup grated parmesan cheese (or more to completely cover top of fish)

½ tsp paprika

lemon wedges and parsley sprigs for garnish

PREPARATION

- Makes about 20 small buffet servings
- Preheat oven to 425-degrees F.
- 45 minutes before your guests arrive, take salmon out of the refrigerator, and allow it to come to room temperature. (You may make prepare the salmon as it

comes to room temperature and simply pop it in the oven 30 minutes before your party.)

- With olive oil, lightly grease a baking dish or sheet pan large enough to accommodate your fillet.
- Season fillet with salt and pepper.
- Slather mayonnaise over top of fillet to cover entirely.
- Sprinkle with parmesan cheese and press into mayonnaise.
- Sprinkle with paprika.
- Bake uncovered for 20 – 25 minutes.

To serve:

With two spatulas, carefully transfer fillet to a pretty serving dish and garnish with lemon wedges and parsley.

JANE GENNERALLI'S CAESAR SALAD

Yields 6 servings

INGREDIENTS

SALAD

2 large heads Romaine lettuce, cleaned

HOMEMADE CROUTONS

4 – 6 slices good white bread cut into 1" cubes

¼ cup extra virgin olive oil

garlic powder

2 TBS grated parmesan cheese (Kraft)

DRESSING

1 coddled egg

2 cloves peeled garlic

(1) 2-ounce tin flat fillets of anchovies, divided

2 – 3 TBS lemon juice

1 TBS Worcestershire sauce

1 TBS Dijon mustard

½ cup grated parmesan cheese (Kraft) or freshly grated Pecorino cheese

Note: To coddle egg: submerge in boiling water and cook for 1 minute. Let cool enough to handle and then immediately crack open and scoop out egg into a blender or food processor.

PREPARATION
CROUTONS

- Preheat oven to 350 degrees F.
- Cut bread slices into 1½" squares and arrange on a baking sheet. Drizzle about ¼ cup olive oil over bread squares. Sprinkle generously with garlic powder and Parmesan cheese. Bake in oven for approximately 10 minutes, checking often to assure the bread doesn't burn. Remove the pan from the oven and flip each bread cube. Return to oven for an additional 5 minutes, or until bread cubes are nicely browned on both sides.

DRESSING

To blender or food processor add coddled egg, garlic, 6 anchovies, lemon juice, mustard, and a generous dash of salt and pepper.

Slowly add remaining olive oil to top of food processer or blender, allowing emulsion to incorporate. (This is where the magic begins, and it won't take but a minute.)

Note: Dressing may be made up to 24 hours before serving.

TO ASSEMBLE SALAD

Tear Romaine leaves into a large wooden salad bowl. Add croutons, shredded cheese, and additional whole anchovies if desired. Just prior to serving, add about ½ cup dressing and toss till Romaine leaves are well coated.

To serve:

Serve in individual salad bowls to your salivating guests.

Note: The leftover dressing may be stored in a small jar or sealed container and will last about 3 days.

AMY SCHADE'S PECAN SANDIES

Makes about 35 cookies

INGREDIENTS:
   1 cup butter, softened
   1/3 cup sugar
   2 tsp vanilla
   2 cups flour
   1 cup chopped pecans
   ¼ cup powdered sugar (plus more)

PREPARATION

- Preheat oven to 325 degrees F
- With an electric mixer, beat butter for 30 seconds.
- Add sugar and beat until fluffy.
- Add vanilla and 2 tsp water and beat well.
- On low-speed mix in flour and pecans.
- Shape into 1-inch balls and place on ungreased baking sheet.
- Bake at 325 degrees for about 15 - 20 minutes.
- Cool completely, then gently roll one at a time in a bowl with powdered sugar to coat.
- Store in airtight containers.

STACY PARKER'S SPRINGERLE COOKIES

Makes about 35 cookies

Springerles are a German cookie traditionally served on holidays and special occasions. They are made with a special rolling pin that has been carved out into simple patterns that impart lovely designs on the dough. Dating back 700 years, springerles have a rich history. When stored in airtight containers in a cool, dry place, springerles can last for a month or longer and get better over time. With their hard outer crust and dense centers, they are often served with and/or dunked in beverages such as hot cocoa, coffee, sweet liquors, or tea. To many, the aroma of the springerle is evocative of Christmas.

INGREDIENTS
  4 eggs
  1 pound (about 4 cups) sifted powdered sugar
  20 drops anise oil
  4 cups sifted flour
  1 tsp baking soda
  anise seed

PREPARATION

- Preheat oven to 300-degrees F.
- With an electric mixer, beat eggs until light and fluffy.
- Slowly add sugar and continue beating on high for 15 minutes until mixture is like soft meringue.
- Add anise oil.
- Sift together flour and soda and blend into sugar mixture on low speed. Dough will be very stiff.
- Cover bowl tightly with tin foil and refrigerate for at least an hour or overnight.
- Divide dough into thirds.
- On lightly floured surface roll each piece into an 8-inch square (about ¼ inch thick).
- Let stand for 1 minute. Dust springerle rolling pin with flour.
- Roll hard enough to make a clear imprint.
- Cut squares apart with sharp knife.
- Place on lightly floured surface, cover with a tea towel and let stand overnight.
- Grease cookie sheets and sprinkle each with anise seed.
- Using fingers, rub underside of each cookie lightly with cold water and place on cookie sheets.
- Bake at 300 degrees F for about 20 minutes or until cookies are a light straw color.
- These get better with age so make ahead and store in airtight containers.

AMY SCHADE'S FINNISH CHESTNUT FINGERS

Makes about 20 cookies

INGREDIENTS:
  1 cup flour
  ¼ tsp cinnamon
  ¼ tsp salt
  6 TBS butter softened
  ¼ cup sugar
  1 egg yolk
  ½ cup chestnut puree or canned chestnuts drained and pureed
  ½ tsp vanilla
  3 oz semisweet chocolate melted and cooled

PREPARATION

- Preheat oven to 350-degrees F.
- Combine flour, cinnamon and ¼ tsp salt, and set aside.
- Beat butter for 30 seconds and add sugar. Beat until fluffy.
- Add egg yolk and beat well. Beat in chestnut puree and vanilla.
- Add dry ingredients and beat well.

- Roll into finger shapes (about 1 rounded TBS rolled 2½ inches long).
- Place on greased cookie sheet and sprinkle with additional sugar.
- Bake at 350 degrees for about 20 minutes until lightly browned.
- When cool dip one end of each finger into melted chocolate and place on wax paper.
- Chill about 10 minutes until chocolate is set.

LIZZY CORKER'S BASIC SUGAR COOKIES

Makes about 25 cookies

INGREDIENTS
  2 cups flour
  1½ tsp baking powder
  ¼ tsp salt
  6 TBS butter, softened
  1/3 cup shortening
  ¾ cup sugar
  1 egg
  1TBS milk
  1 tsp vanilla

PREPARATION

- Preheat oven to 375 degrees F.
- Stir together dry ingredients and set aside.
- Beat together butter and shortening about 30 seconds. Add sugar and beat until fluffy. Add egg, milk and vanilla and beat well.
- Add dry ingredients and beat until well blended.
- Cover and chill at least 3 hours.

- Divide dough in half and roll to about 1/8 inch thick on a lightly floured surface.
- Cut with cookie cutters and bake at 375 degrees F on ungreased cookie sheet for 8 minutes.
- Decorate.

Note: Traditionally, a very thin frosting consisting of powdered sugar and milk beaten with an electric mixer is used to glaze these cookies. Frost each cookie one at a time, and then decorate with colored sugars and/or candy sprinkles before the frosting sets. This is a wonderful family project; Mom or Dad can frost the cookies and the children can decorate them.

ERIC BARONE'S SINFUL CHOCOLATE COOKIES

Makes about 30 cookies

INGREDIENTS
- 1 cup butter
- ¾ cup granulated sugar
- ¾ cup brown sugar
- 2 eggs
- 2 ½ cups flour
- 1 tsp baking powder
- 1½ tsp baking soda
- ½ tsp salt
- 1 cup cocoa powder
- 1 bar Bakers Sweet Chocolate
- ½ cup strong coffee (Leftover from breakfast works just fine.)

PREPARATION

- Preheat oven to 350-degrees F.
- In a large bowl, cream butter and sugars until light and fluffy.
- Beat in eggs with a hand mixer.

- In a medium size bowl combine flour, baking powder, baking soda, salt and cocoa powder and stir until well blended.
- Add half of flour mixture to butter mixture and stir to incorporate, and then repeat with the remaining flour mixture.
- Add coffee a tablespoon at a time until flour mixture is absorbed. (You may not need the entire ½ cup of coffee. Use only what you need to get a very dense batter that holds together.)
- Break the chocolate bar into pieces and process in a food processor until crumbly with some chunks and add to mix.
- Drop by tsp onto ungreased cookie sheets, forming little mounds.
- Bake 8 – 10 minutes.
- Let cookies rest for 2 minutes on cookie sheets before removing to wire racks to cool completely.

MAGGIE JENKIN'S FLAKEY PASTRY CRUST

Makes 2 single pie crusts

INGREDIENTS
2½ cups all-purpose flour, plus extra for rolling
1 cup (2 sticks) very cold unsalted butter, cut into approx. ½" pieces
1 tsp salt
1 tsp sugar
6 to 8 TBS ice water
1 egg white
1 additional TBS sugar

Variation:
Swap out ½ cup of the flour with ground blanched almonds or almond flour

PREPARATION

- Place butter in the freezer. Mix the first four dry ingredients in a food processor till combined.
- Add the frozen butter in bits and pieces and process in batches until incorporated. (The trick here is to not over-process and keep the mix cool.)

- Drizzle in the water a tsp at a time and process until the mixture is very crumbly but holds together when compressed.
- Turn the dough out onto a cutting board and press it into a mass.
- Divide the dough into two equal portions, form into two balls, and flatten into discs. Wrap discs in plastic wrap and refrigerate for 4 hours or up to three days.
- On a lightly flour-dusted surface and using a floured rolling pin, roll out the dough into two 12" X 1/8" circles. Either transfer one crust to a 9" pie pan, fold the edges over, crimp and fill with your pie filling and reserve the other for another one-crust pie, or use both rounds in a two-crust pie.

MAGGIE JENKIN'S BERRY PIE FILLING

Makes 1 pie

INGREDIENTS

1-quart fresh berries (raspberries, blueberries or blackberries, or a combination)

1½ cup granulated sugar

1/3 cup cornstarch

1 TBS Sure-Jell pectin or minute tapioca

2 TBS lemon juice

PREPARATION

- Preheat oven to 425-degree F.
- Combine sugar, cornstarch, pectin or Minute Tapioca.
- Add berries and lemon juice and let sit for 15 minutes (while rolling out the pie crusts).
- Put berries in the bottom crust, fit top crust over filling, and crimp edges.
- Make slits in the top crust to allow steam to escape.
- Bake in a 425-degree F oven for 15 minutes and then lower the temperature to 300-degrees F and continue baking for another 25 – 35 minutes until the juices are bubbling add the crust is turning a light golden brown.

STACY PARKER'S FRESH PEACH PIE

Makes 2 single or (1) 2-crust pie

INGREDIENTS
- 2 unbaked pie crust rounds (top and bottom)
- 4 cups washed peaches, pitted, unpeeled, and cut into pieces
- 2 TBS fresh lemon juice
- 1 cup granulated sugar
- ½ cup brown sugar
- ½ tsp cinnamon
- ¼ cup cornstarch
- ½ tsp salt

PREPARATION

- Preheat oven to 425-degrees F.
- In a medium size bowl, add lemon juice to peaches and mix gently.
- Combine sugars in another medium-sized bowl. Then, add cornstarch, salt, and cinnamon and mix well.
- Add sugar/cornstarch mixture to peaches and stir to blend.
- Pour filling into unbaked pie shell and top with second crust.

- Crimp edges of crusts and brush top crust with egg (white) wash, sprinkle with 1 TBS granulated sugar, and dot with bits of butter.
- Cut one or more slits into the top crust to allow steam to vent (or use a cookie cutter to create a pretty design).
- Bake in a 425-degree F oven for 10 minutes—placing a baking sheet on the rack below your pie to catch any juices.
- Turn the temperature down to 350-degrees F and continue baking for another 35 - 45 minutes or until the crust is light golden brown and juices are bubbling from the vents.
- Serve while still warm with vanilla ice cream.

CELIA HAWTHORNE'S FRESH APPLE PIE FILLING

Makes about 5 cups

INGREDIENTS

    4 cups apples peeled, cored, and sliced
    Juice of 1/2 a lemon
    3 cups water
    1 1/3 cup granulated sugar
    1/3 cup cornstarch
    1 tsp cinnamon
    ¼ tsp salt
    ¼ tsp nutmeg

PREPARATION

- Place apples in a large bowl and toss with lemon juice.
- Place water, sugar, cornstarch, cinnamon, salt, and nutmeg in a medium saucepan.
- Stir to combine, then bring to a boil over medium heat, stirring often.
- Let mixture come to a boil, and boil for two minutes.
- Add the apples and reduce heat to a simmer.
- Cook, stirring often, until the apples soften, about 5-8 minutes.

- Pour into mason jars, cool to room temperature, and then cover and refrigerate or freeze.

Note: The mixture will thicken as it cools. If freezing, do not tightly fasten lids until filling is completely frozen as it will expand and, potentially, overflow and make a mess in your freezer.

Don't miss out on your next favorite book!

Join the Satin Romance mailing list
www.satinromance.com/mail.html

THANK YOU FOR READING

Did you enjoy this book?

We invite you to leave a review at your favorite book site, such as
Goodreads, Amazon, Barnes & Noble, etc.

DID YOU KNOW THAT LEAVING A REVIEW...

- Helps other readers find books they may enjoy.
- Gives you a chance to let your voice be heard.
- Gives authors recognition for their hard work.
- Doesn't have to be long. A sentence or two about why
  you liked the book will do.

ABOUT THE AUTHOR

Award winning author of the gripping memoir, *Dancing with the Devil*, and the children's book, *Dune Dragons*. Gretchen Rose spent most of her adult life operating a high-end interior design firm in Vero Beach, FL. A classically trained soprano, she has performed in countless professional musical and theatrical venues and penned four musical comedies. Gretchen's love of music and theater colors all her writing. She is currently at work on an historical fantasy novel set in San Antonio's Japanese Tea Garden.

www.gretchenroseauthor.com
www.gretchenroseauthor.com/blog

facebook.com/Gretchen-Rose-Author-2163047320474640
instagram.com/rose_gretchen

ALSO BY GRETCHEN ROSE

With Satin Romance

<u>Novels</u>

A Christmas Charm

With Melange Books

<u>Very Vero</u>

Veni Vidi Vero

A Little Vice in Vero